TRINAL

PAX SINCLAIR

ISBN: 978-1-7336445-3-2 (Print Edition)
ISBN-13: 978-1-7336445-2-5 (ebook Edition)

Printed and bound in the United States of America
First printing November 2019

Red Kettle Ink

Published by Red Kettle Ink
2010 El Camino Real #1151
Santa Clara, CA 95050

www.paxsinclair.com

Book Cover by Uniquely Tailored
www.uniquelytailored.com

Table of Contents

CHAPTER 1

Folio

"What are you willing to gamble, steal, or throw away for love?"

"Shelby." I looked up to see Ana, my administrative assistant, entering my office. "They're all in the executive conference room. The committees have just begun the swearing in."

"Thank you, I'm right behind you," I said, trying to find my heels underneath the desk. I slipped them on, stood while adjusting my skirt, grabbed my laptop, and walked out of my office.

I'd been at Folio since I was seventeen, the first year of my internship with the company. Shy and studious, I couldn't believe I'd landed a job at my dream company.

Fidgeting in my seat while waiting for orientation to begin with five other lucky interns, it all seemed like a fantasy, as I remember. Carter Morrison, the handsome, larger-than-life CEO of Folio, strolled in to welcome us to the company and at that moment I instantly transformed into a hopeless lovesick tart. I wanted this god to notice me and did everything I could to be close to him, short of taking all my clothes off and sprawling naked on his desk to get his attention. Which I did happily a year later.

To Carter's credit, he never touched me until the night I turned eighteen. He confessed later that he did everything he could to stay away from me that first year.

The leadership team, my communication group of four, and a couple of the attorneys from Legal filled the executive conference room. We were watching the Judiciary and Commerce Committee's joint hearing on C-SPAN from Washington. Carter Morrison was at the table with four other industry powerhouses answering questions on the latest consumer complaints on privacy practices of social media companies. Carter sat in the middle of the table in a custom steel-gray suit that highlighted the touch of gray in his coal-black hair. Blue eyes crinkled into fine lines when he flashed his signature smile. He'd just completed his explanation of our protocols, directing the information to Senator Watson, who'd asked the question. Even I could see she had difficulties not appearing to be dazzled by Carter.

The CEO of Folio was a walking legend. There were other executives around the table, all in expensive suits, but they were boys and girls compared to him. This was The Carter Show. Rugged good looks at forty-eight, a hard body and, oh, that swagger that turned heads when he walked into the room, he was charisma personified. Two seconds into his orbit and you would've done anything for him too. For a woman, it was that soft Tennessee drawl. If you weren't careful, it would charm the clothes right off of you.

The atmosphere in the conference room was cautious camaraderie. Someone had provided a breakfast buffet. Later, lunch and eventually dinner would be served. Most of the group seated around the table were drinking coffee and taking notes. It would be a long day. Some senate hearings lasted up to ten hours.

It was an elaborate necessary theater for the cameras, something legislators used to placate public outcry to show the voters they were doing something. The hearing was real, but not the adversarial atmosphere in the room. Carter knew everyone on the committees personally. He'd helped to shape much of the regulations for his industry. We'd pick up after the hearings ended; Legal would craft more policies on privacy, tweaking them to our advantage. We were in the information business to make money. Folio would launch a new ad campaign, the kind that made us nostalgic and relevant to our users. Our customers would forget to turn on the new privacy settings, continue to enjoy our products, and life would go on.

CHAPTER 2

Cabbages and Kings

Carter was holding court in his office, an executive suite with views on three sides of Silicon Valley. He'd lost his suit jacket and tie somewhere between the plane and here. He wore a light grey slim-fit cotton shirt, the sleeves rolled up to the elbows, exposing his tanned, well-developed forearms, looking more like a blue-collar boss than a high-powered CEO. His black hair wasn't slicked back; he was more casual. This was my favorite look for him, what he normally looked like at the end of the day.

Leaning back in his chair at the head of the table, his pen tapped out an impatient series of staccato beats while listening to the General Counsel suggest we all review the seven-hour tape of his testimony again. But an irritated Carter was having none of it. "I don't need to see the tape. Good God damn, I was there. What I need is data!" His soft Tennessee voice was more prominent when irritated. "I want to know the results from the overnight polling and the focus group data. When I was coming back on the plane last night," he was speaking to everyone around the table, "you told me you had finished compiling the information and it would be available for this meeting."

Chad, the youngest of my team and the most ambitious member, rummaged through paperwork then glanced at his screen. He had requested to lead this discussion. He'd managed the focus groups and gathered the data. It was appropriate that I grant him this opportunity to lead. I just hoped Carter wouldn't leave bite marks on his behind.

I sat on the couch and allowed him to take my place at the table with the rest of the executive team. He puffed up, looking like a peacock about to pop out his feathers, when he began his presentation.

"We just received the raw data but haven't had a chance to analyze the numbers." He hazarded a glance at Carter, who gave him a get-on-with-it Mount Rushmore stare. Chad, like the overconfident little shit he was, who had been gunning for my job since day one, brushed it off and pushed through the rebuke. "It seems your favorability has dropped a bit, but that was only at the beginning of your testimony at the hearing. By the end we noted the numbers had seen a small but encouraging uptick. What I can say, without really plowing through the numbers, is that you're somewhere between dead even in favorability or a little better. We still have those zealots who are canceling their accounts and announcing it to anyone who will listen, but the percentage of people following that mode is significantly less than a third of a quarter percent. In my opinion, I don't think they will make much of an impact."

Carter looked around the room at his team. We were the best at what we did or we wouldn't be here. There were no free rides at Folio; you earned a spot at this table. We were an easygoing, close-knit group, but sometimes Carter ruled his company with an iron fist. The stare he gave us today was serious and felt by every member sitting in this room. "What you're saying is the impact from these hearings was minimal?"

I spoke up. "What Chad was saying is that it's too early to tell. We need to let this sit with the public to see what the fallout will be. That means watching the media to see how much they want to push this issue." What I was really saying is that we hoped that consumer watchdog reporters like Sagan Miller would not take up the cause and fan the flames. "As a precautionary measure, I've invited Sagan and a few other local news outlets for a conference at Folio's headquarters to discuss the hearings. We need to drive home that we are serious about working on this issue and have nothing to hide."

Sagan was at the top of my list of things to be worried about. He'd gained his reporting chops in places like Washington DC and New York. Before arriving in Silicon Valley, he'd already gained a reputation. His notoriety and his ability to break controversial news stories made him feared and revered in the tech community.

Carter had no fear of Sagan, unlike his other colleagues. I'd only seen the two men together once at a cocktail party. It was rare that Carter and I would be in a public place together. They'd invited the executive team to a ceremony honoring Carter. Sagan attended and, although it was only for a few minutes, the two seemed to have an easiness in each other's company. Most of my contact with Sagan was through my work with Folio. Carter insisted I contact him if we had to get ahead of a not-too-flattering story or if we needed to leak information anonymously to the public.

"Boys and girls, that's enough for today," Carter said and tossed his pen on the table. "I took the red-eye in and I'm planning to work a couple more hours, then go home. But I'll hit it bright and early tomorrow and I expect to see all of you in the sandbox as well."

I closed my laptop and got ready to file out with the rest of the team to finish the pile of work I had sitting on my desk.

"Hey, Shelby." I looked up at Alec, the head of Legal. He was a tall, gentle giant who always made time for me when I had legal questions. In fact, I was the one that introduced him to Jordan, his wife. "Jordan said thank you for the baby shower gift. She also said you didn't need to send gifts to the kids, but it's appreciated, and she will take you up on that spa day with you after the baby is here. But I really wanted to thank you for the romantic weekend at that Half Moon Bay Resort as a present to the soon-to-be sleep-deprived parents of a new baby. If that wasn't enough, you offered to babysit our three little hellions for that weekend while we're gone. I want to say if no one has put you up for sainthood, I'm willing to do it."

"No problem," I laughed, "It's the least I can do for the first assistant I had when I became Director of Communications. I can't tell you how many times Jordan saved my bacon. As for your three little angels, I'm looking forward to spending the weekend with them."

"Shelby, will you stay for a few minutes?" Carter's weary voice cut through our conversation. "I have a few more questions about the data Chad presented in the meeting."

Alec looked over his shoulder at his boss, then back at me. In a whisper that Carter could hear, he said, "Don't stay too long talking to this old dragon. He'll have you working all night if he thinks you'll do it."

"Alec," Carter's voice rumbled with fake irritation, "you've been skating on thin ice with me for the last five years. If you weren't such a brilliant goddamn attorney, I would have fired your ass a long time ago. But since Jordan and Shelby, two women who are above reproach but have questionable loyalties, think highly of you, I tolerate you and keep you around only for them."

Alec chuckled. "Remember what I said," he said, winking at me. He took unhurried strides to the door, but just before he walked through to the hallway he stopped and threw another glance at Carter. "You'd better be good to her or you'll answer to me." I thought he was kidding but there seemed to be some seriousness to his words.

Carter frowned, dismissing him. "Your wife is waiting."

The door closed. I slipped my laptop back onto my lap, opening it to search for the file on the committee hearing notes. I looked up at Carter; he was gazing out the window, thinking. "Or do you want to go through all the polling data we received?" I said, "I know you like to crunch the raw numbers yourself..."

He leaned back in his chair. "Not right now. I'm not up to it." He exhaled a frustrated sigh, looking out at the view. "Lord knows those people are taking it right out of me. But I'm home now and that's all that counts." He directed a predatory grin at me. "Come over here. You know what I need."

I pushed the computer off my lap, walking the few steps to his desk. He moved his chair away from the table, padding its surface with his hand. Vivid blue eyes appraised me as I tossed my dark locks back. I moved my hips a little slower, giving him a show. I reached for the top button of my shirt as I perched on the table. I popped one open when Carter reached for my hands, nudging them aside to take charge of opening the rest. Cold air caressed my skin when he pulled the halves of my shirt apart. I arched my back, tempting him with my breasts in red lace. He frowned, running his fingers along the base of the cups. "I know you're a big girl, but I still don't like those whale bones keeping you up."

I nearly guffawed before I caught myself. "It's called an underwire," I smiled. "Jeezes, Carter. You're not that old." Something fluttered across his face. But he recovered quickly, and that lecherous smile returned. I crossed my legs and leaned back on my hand. "Don't you want these double Ds perky and ready?"

He continued to inspect me. "You're only twenty-eight. Why don't you try going without your underwire for a day?"

I frowned at him. He pinched my nipple. "Ouch." I slapped his hand. "Yes, I can see it now. My going without a bra would cause a riot in the halls. You know I can't do that."

He chuckled, "Yeah, you're right. I wanted to see Legal get a group hard-on. He pressed his fingers over the lace then reached his big hand inside the cup and pulled me out, exposing my breast. I placed my hand on his arms, massaging his biceps. I groaned when his thumb drew light circles, brushing my exposed nipple. "Do you like that, baby?" His voice was a low rumble. "Do you want more?"

"Ah huh," I sighed. The pleasure of his touch was like a drug moving slow and intoxicating through my veins. "Are you going to make me beg for it tonight?" I said, lulling into the pleasure of his hand.

He stood up, continuing his light tease, looking into my eyes. "A little begging never hurt anyone."

My pulse raced when he increased the pressure. He had a self-satisfying grin on his handsome face as he watched me. *The little beast knows I want this too much; he's going to make me work for it.* "Do I have the bastard Carter tonight?" I asked.

He squeezed. "Listen, woman, be grateful I don't make you do it on your knees." The words came out like silk. "Now let's hear some conciliatory tones."

I scrunched up my face at him. "Please, Carter. Please fuck me hard or at least do something really nasty to me."

Carter's eyes sparked, trying to suppress a laugh. "You know, Princess, I could probably play with these perfect tits and get you off that way," he said, sliding a hand between my legs, his fingers brushing lightly against the silk of my panties. "Just as I suspected... you're soaked, you dirty little girl."

"Carter," I said, irritated at his teasing, "Are you going to do something or are you going to rely on that Tennessee twang to get me to orgasm?"

He removed his hand from between my legs and considered. "Princess is testy tonight. I guess you missed me."

I wanted to wipe that self-satisfied grin off his face. "Maybe I missed that big cock of yours, but not your stupid humor or that overblown ego."

He placed a lock of my hair behind my ear and brushed my lips. "Stop your complaining, baby," he soothed, "you ain't gotta be nowhere. Come on, talk to me." His hand slid down my thigh, trying to irritate me even more with that down-home come-on.

"Okay," I huffed. "What do you want for your birthday?" I said, trying not to concentrate on his hands at play. "Or have you forgotten it's in a few days? When am I going to get your list?"

He considered. "I thought after all this time you'd be tired of that list."

"Isn't that what we agreed? After that first year together?"

"If it will make you happy, the third item on the list hasn't changed." He grinned, giving me a light squeeze. His hand fell away, his hot mouth on my nipple. The remnants of his day-old beard scratched lightly against my tender skin. He eased me back onto the cold, hard surface of the table, my head making contact with a light thump. The discomfort was the least of it as he shifted partially on top of me, his cock hard through the fabric of his pants. I was too busy concentrating on his insistent mouth, while his hand pulled at the fabric of my bra, tearing the flimsy lace to free my other breast. He squeezed and pinched, the sensation flooding my body. I took a breath, burying my fingers in his hair. His hand held me as he sucked, the other searching under my skirt. His fingers slipped roughly under my silk panties, running a finger through my moisture, then pushing a finger inside.

"I want your cock inside me," I whispered. "Let me unzip you."

"We'll get to that, I promise. All night on the plane ride over here I thought about you and all the things I would do to you when I got you alone."

He'd probably wanted to make it quick and dirty for his first night back with me. That was okay; this was foreplay, and as long as he would stay with me for a few hours we could explore, and I'd work out some of my own sexy daydreams. He was always hard after meetings in his office. It was a turn-on for him to fuck me on the table where he'd just met with his executive team. We'd done it several times before. Once he had me stripped naked and on the table before we heard the last of the team's footfalls down the hall. I didn't care how he wanted me. I'd do it on a subway rumbling down the track with passengers watching as long as it was with him. I relaxed and enjoyed the sensation of his lips on my nipple and his finger inside me. He moved to my side, continuing to tease me with his finger as he settled on his elbow.

"Put another finger inside me, Carter, make it deep."

"Damn, you're wet," he said, and another finger pushed inside. He watched me writhe when his thumb rubbed my clit. "Come on my fingers, Princess, and make it loud. I didn't soundproof this office for you to come with a whimper." I closed my eyes, concentrating on the sensations. He was stroking my hair. "Do it now; I've got more dirty things planned for you," he breathed in my ear. He spread his fingers, moving them slowly. "I'm not going to let you sleep. I'm going to fuck you all night." I arched my back and screamed.

"Good girl." His fingers pulled out of me. His approval made me want more of our naughty play. "You're sexy when you let go."

I kissed him, glad that he was back after a week away. If he'd stayed longer, I would have taken personal time and flown to Washington.

Carter brushed a lock of my hair from my cheek. He said he'd be with me all night. He was right, I wouldn't sleep. I wouldn't take my hands off of him.

"Princess." He held up two fingers slick with my musky fluid. I smiled. "Suck." He instructed. I did, greedily, cleaning my essence from him. He brushed his thumb over my chin. "I could watch you come all night."

The phone rang next to my head. We both stared at each other for a few seconds. It rang again. I broke the spell, rolled over onto my side, and pressed the button. "Carter?" Ana's voice boomed unnaturally through the speaker, "Is Shelby with you?"

Carter motioned he was going to his apartment. I sat up.

"I'm sorry to bother you. But she asked me to hunt her down if Sagan Miller called." That was Ana, my concerned admin.

"I'm here," I said. "What happened?"

"Sagan was irritated when he found out I couldn't put him through to you right away." That was Mr. Miller. If he didn't get what he wanted immediately, he lost interest. Until he remembered he wanted it again. My usually unruffled admin sounded worried. "He says he'll wait for a few minutes, but he's waiting on his source to call him back. He can't promise how long he'll be available. What should I tell him?"

"Tell him not to get his undies in a twist, that I'm just finishing up a meeting and I'll be right there."

"I'll tell him. Do you remember that I'm going to a function with my husband tonight in the city? I have to leave now if we're going to get there on time."

I felt awful. That's why she was still in the office. She should've been gone a long time ago. "Yes, I remember. Just put him on hold after you tell him I'm coming and go. I don't want you to be late. Oh, and Ana, please don't tell him I referred to his twisted undies."

"No problem."

Carter returned with a washcloth and towel. "Here, you can clean up with this."

"Thanks." The warm, wet cloth felt good.

Carter looked out at the lights of the valley. "You told Sagan that you needed to speak with him. Should I be worried?"

I placed the towels in a pile. "Looks like you got new towels for the compartment," I said.

He nodded. That was the nickname we called the executive suite's attached two-bedroom apartment. "They repainted while I was gone. They even gave me new linens."

I buttoned my blouse and stuffed the tail into my waistband. He kissed me on the forehead and I moved off the table. "Remember, at the meeting, I announced the invitation to Sagan and a few other news outlets in the valley for a mini press conference at Folio. I've called him a few times to invite him personally, because you know how he is, but Mr. Ace Reporter is difficult to catch. I asked Ana to find me if he called back." I moved away from the table, straightening my skirt and running quick fingers through my hair just in case I met anyone between here and my office. I walked by the couch to pick up my laptop.

The chair leather crackled as he adjusted. "Don't take too long; I'd like to talk to you tonight."

I was going to say, "You need to finish what you started," but something stopped me when the tiredness in his face returned. Maybe it was testifying in Washington that was bothering him, but we'd been through worse and he always came out on the other end unscathed. I'd know soon enough after my phone call.

"Remember to send me your birthday list," I said, "I want it by tomorrow." He nodded. I blew him a kiss and walked out of his office.

"Have you called because you decided you want my body and can't wait any longer?" Sagan's voice sounded distant. Was everyone in a mood tonight? I pictured him resting his phone on his cheek, writing something, while I was talking to him, that ever-present smirk on his face and no shirt. I just improvised that last bit. My time with Carter had me keyed up.

I'd met Sagan a few times over the last several years. To say he was a big, strapping lad would be an understatement. He was well over 6 feet tall and had the tenacity of a bulldog in heat. But he also had a disarming charm and when he directed it to you, you had difficulty remembering what zip code you lived in. I suspected that was how he got most of his exclusive stories.

We first met on a warm, rainy day. I was in a coffee shop, sipping cappuccino, with my trusty compact umbrella by my side waiting for an industry association meeting to begin. Sagan sauntered in, without a jacket, soaked to the bone, his white cotton shirt sticking artfully to his well-defined chest. He looked like a god who had decided to slum the day on Earth instead of being fed grapes by nymphs on Mount Olympus. He grabbed a coffee from the counter and, to my horror and delight, the only open seat was at my table. He raked his fingers through his black locks, wiped off his right hand, stuck it out, and introduced himself. "Hi, I'm Sagan Miller and you're Shelby Oberman. I've seen you before; sorry I waited this long to talk to you."

That was the beginning of our little cat-and-mouse game. He'd flirt, and I'd say no or ignore his suggestions. I accepted his coffee invitations a few times, but I stopped. He was a shrewd reporter, and the encounters left me hot and bothered. Carter was actually the winner after those meetings. I was extra horny and he got the benefit. "Shelby, you there? Or are you picturing yourself in my bed?"

"We can talk about that another time," I teased.

"Really?" I heard something clatter to the ground in the background.

"Don't get excited. I'm inviting you to our headquarters for a press conference. It'll give you a chance to ask Carter questions about the privacy hearings."

"Is this an exclusive with Carter?"

I changed the phone to my other ear and pushed off my shoes. Those pointy heels would be the death of me. "No, it's a press conference. I'm inviting some of your other colleagues to the party as well."

"You haven't given me an answer about that exclusive I proposed. I want to do a profile on you. The woman behind the man?"

"There's no story to tell. I'm just the communications director, not a kingmaker. Unless you want to talk about my knitting addiction, then we don't have much to talk about."

"We'll talk one day; I have no doubt. But in the meantime, text me the information on the press conference and I'll make room on my calendar to be there."

After my chat with Sagan, I traced my steps back to Carter's office. The place was quiet this late in the evening; no one was around. When I reached the door, I swiped my badge and pushed through, but found no Carter inside. I was about to check the compartment when I saw a note sitting in the middle of his desk. *I had to go. We'll talk later, and I'll finish what I started.*

CHAPTER 3

Cut Zone

he next day, I was on the phone talking to a magazine editor about the details of an article they wanted to run on Folio and its CEO when Ana walked into my office holding a sign. The black Sharpie message read: *You need to get off the phone. Carter is on a rampage. He wants you in his office now!*

"What the fuck..." I mumbled.

"What did you say, Shelby?"

"Sorry, a minor catastrophe just cropped up." Thank God I'd known Melinda for a long time. I attempted to finish the conversation while Ana motioned for me to hurry it up. I covered the receiver. "Tell Carter I'm on my way," I said, giving her a scooting motion, and resumed the conversation. "Yeah, no problem. We can do that, but we'll need to have advertising in the issue as well... No, we can talk terms later... Unfortunately, I have another meeting to run to. But we can have coffee soon." I put the receiver down. Ana frowned, folding her makeshift poster.

"What's going on?" I asked, searching for my heels under my desk. "Why is he demanding to see me?" I look toward the door. "Did something go wrong with the committee hearings? Are they requesting we come back?"

"He only wants to talk to you and Alec. He didn't tell me anything, just that you need to get to his office right away."

I raced down the hall and veered left, almost crashing into one of the new interns. I barreled into Carter's office, my feet aching from my sprint in heels. Carter was at his desk. Alec sat on the couch. Both men were grim-faced and looking at the TV mounted on the wall. *Cut Zone*, a celebrity gossip tabloid show, was on the screen. Two plastic people were in an animated conversation with a picture of Carter in the background. "What's this...?"

"Shush, sit down and listen," Alec said without taking his gaze from the screen.

The blonde woman, who I'd seen before, was the gossip queen on the show. She sat with a young manscaped male at a table. The set simulated two friends talking or gossiping. "Diana," the young man said, "which celeb has made the cut and is in the zone today?"

The woman looked away from her companion and straight into the camera. "The CEO of Folio is in more hot water. Lately he's been on the hot seat testifying at a senate hearing in Washington, which we all watched because he was the star witness in those dull proceedings. He's just returned to Silicon Valley when he's hit with another problem close to home. Hunky CEO Carter Morrison, who could give Gerard Butler a serious run for his money..."

At that moment, they flashed a picture of Gerard and Carter at a charity event looking like they could be related. "Yum, right, ladies? Court filings today revealed that Cecile Morrison, wife of Carter Morrison, has filed for divorce and has named Shelby Oberman as the party that alienated her husband's affections. We've obtained a photograph of Carter and Shelby together. This picture was used as evidence of the affair."

A grainy black-and-white photograph appeared. The man, tall and broad-shouldered, was dressed in an overcoat. The camera caught him in quarter profile, his hand at the small of the woman's back. More of her face was visible, and the woman in the photo was me. "That was a surprise?" she cooed. "We all thought it would be the Italian model Jozelle Botticelli. But no, he found something more interesting close to home. Ms. Oberman is the Director of Communications at Folio."

My awful corporate photo came up on the screen. The one that made me look like I had a stick up my ass. "He got it in his own backyard." She sighed and gave the camera a you-could-have-done-way-better smile. "I'll keep you informed, ladies. But my suggestion is that you bitches better get in line, because Carter Morrison is back on the market."

Alec pressed the remote, and the screen went blank. He turned a worried attorney face to me. "I got a ten-minute warning they were airing this piece from a friend who works at the network. We need to get ready for a barrage of press over this. It doesn't help that twenty reporters will be here in two hours to fire questions at Carter about the privacy hearings. More than likely there will be little to no questions about the hearings and more on the divorce."

Carter hadn't turned away from the TV. He hadn't even acknowledged that I was in the room. What was going on in that calculating brain of his? Alec turned to Carter. "Do you have any suggestions?"

Carter swung his attention to Alec. "I thought that was your department."

"I can strategize a hundred possibilities, but it would help if you could tell me what direction you're planning to move."

"I think you should get back to your office and think up a few scenarios we can discuss later."

"Is that your subtle way of telling me to get out of here?" Alec looked at me. "I get it, the two of you have a lot to talk about." He headed for the door. "Let me know when we can talk. I've already got a few ideas on how this can go down."

I'd never spoken to Carter about his relationship with Cecile. He'd always kept us separate. Truth was, I never wanted to know.

"I'm sorry you had to hear about the divorce like this," Carter said. "She's been threatening to divorce me for a while now, but I never thought she would do it." Then it hit me: he was free now. This wasn't the best way to start, but after the scandal died down, we could have a real relationship. Carter put his arms around me and I leaned into him. "Shelby, about all this. I was going to talk to you yesterday when I came in from Washington, but you distracted me." He gave me a squeeze. "It doesn't matter now. Unfortunately, we don't have time to talk. Everything will be alright. I need you to trust me. It's a lot to ask, but can you do that?"

I let out the breath I was holding and nodded. Carter was a master at chaos management. Just when you thought we were on the brink of disaster; he'd always pull it out and made it look easy. "Of course, Carter, anything you need. But we need to craft a statement for the press."

"I'm working on it with Alec. I need someone who isn't personally involved to help me. Right now, you're up to your eyeballs in alligators. In the meantime, give a no-comment to the press or anyone else."

"Should I cancel the press conference? We'll be better prepared if we have a day."

"No, having a press conference in the next couple of hours is probably the best thing for us." He moved to get his jacket.

"Where are you going? I thought Alec was coming back here for your meeting."

"I have to run off campus to check something. I'll be back as soon as possible. Tell Alec to keep working on that statement. I expect it to be perfect by the time I knock on his door. He reached for me and softly kissed my lips. "I love you, Shelby Oberman. Remember that."

I sat in my office with my head in my hands, wondering about the next several hours. Ana appeared at the door with two cups of coffee. She set one cup on my desk. "I have nothing stronger, so this will have to do. I think you're going to need something to get through this," she said as she moved to the couch.

"Out there," I motioned toward the general office. It was eerily deserted on my walk back to my office. "How bad was it?"

"On a scale from one to ten? I'd say about a hundred. I watched the announcement. Someone must have seen the intro on *Cut Zone* that there would be some juicy gossip about Carter, so word got around. That's how I heard about it. I would say everyone on the floor was jammed into the breakroom gawking at the TV."

"What did they say?" I didn't want to know the answer, but I was still curious.

"Half of them were shocked. The other half said they suspected it. I don't believe it for one minute. You never go out in public together unless it's in a group."

Ana knew about Carter and me. Jordan, my first admin, did too. It was hard to hide anything from your administrative assistant. But both women were discreet. I always suspected Alec, Jordon's husband, might have known. I was sure of it after that comment in Carter's office yesterday. "You're right. We never go out in public together. So how did they get that photo?"

"What are you going to say?" She took a sip.

"Carter suggested I give no comment, which is the best way to go right now. It's better if he addresses the divorce filing first. I wish I knew more about that or what he's planning."

"You didn't know anything about this?"

"I found out the same way you did, from that *Cut Zone* broadcast. I talked with Carter briefly. He said Cecile had been threatening a divorce, but he never thought she'd go through with it."

"Are you going to deny the affair? That man in the photo couldn't possibly be Carter, unless they have other evidence."

I wasn't sure. The shot was too tightly cropped to establish where we were. The picture might have been taken some distance away; it looked like a surveillance photo. Without talking this out with Carter, it was difficult to decide what to do. I wasn't sure I should even attend the press conference today. Questions would be directed at Carter, but there was nothing to stop the reporters from asking me uncomfortable questions.

I wondered if I had enough goodwill with Sagan to talk with him about this. "I'm calling Sagan. Maybe I can pull in a favor and find out his take on this mess. I'm sure he's heard the news by now."

Ana stood up. "I'll leave you to it then. Let me know if I need to do something. I've already started fielding calls, and I've told them you have no comment."

The phone rang for a long time before he picked up. "The woman of the hour, calling me," Sagan said, "I knew my instincts were right about you and there was more going on."

"I'm calling to find out how much of a story this will be in the press."

"This is big, huge big. Not only is Folio in hot water for violating their customers' privacy, but now their CEO has a big juicy scandal brewing. I'm not going to lie; they see blood in the water."

"It's not what you think."

"What do I think?"

I said nothing, just kept chewing my lip.

"Why don't you give me that exclusive I've been asking about?" He was turning on that famous charm. "Better yet, why not a live interview? I can do a piece on you and Carter together or separately. At least you could get your stories out there accurately."

That would be a big help. But at this point I didn't know what game Carter was playing. "Can I get back to you on that?"

"Sure, but don't wait too long. If I'm first out of the gate with a substantive piece, it could help you and me."

"Are you coming to our press conference?" I asked. If I did decide to attend, at least Sagan would be a supportive face.

"Other than aliens capturing me and using my body for research, I wouldn't miss it for the world."

CHAPTER 4

One-Ring Circus

I didn't attend the press conference. We decided to keep the focus on Carter. Security escorted the press to a small auditorium in the meeting center on our campus. I was viewing a private feed in my office with Ana, who was sitting on my couch with her third cup of coffee.

Alec appeared from a side entrance and walked to the podium. "My name is Alec Dunakin, Chief Legal Officer at Folio. Thank you for attending this press conference at our headquarters. Carter Morrison will be here shortly to read a brief statement, then afterward he will answer your questions." Alec left the podium and took a seat in the front row with the executive team.

The camera remained on the empty podium, the familiar Folio logo prominent on the lectern's front. There were about three rows of press, speaking with hushed voices, waiting for Carter to appear. I wasn't sure if Carter was held up or if he was milking his entrance. I would bet that it was probably a little bit of both. The door in back of the podium opened and Carter strode forward. Freshly shaven and immaculate in a dark navy suit, he adjusted the microphone up.

"Good afternoon." Carter's voice boomed over the assembly. "I want to read a brief statement and then I'll take your questions." He looked at the audience, a ghost of a smile on his lips. "Before I read my prepared remarks, I want to say that we invited you here to ask questions about the privacy hearings in Washington. And I'm eager to discuss our participation in the hearings and our vision moving forward. However, since the story about my pending divorce hit the news, I am under no illusions that you are actually here for more information about that topic." A titter of laughter rose from the room. "I would like to make a statement about the news story and then I will answer your questions. If you still have questions about the privacy hearings, I would be happy to talk about that as well."

Carter pulled a sheet of paper from his breast pocket, placing it on the lectern, studying the sheet for a second. The room was waiting in silence. Looking up, he scanned the sea of faces, then left the podium to stand in front. That was a bold move to leave the protection of the podium, but that was a classic Carter move. He stood, not cowered or contrite; he was just Carter. "I was unaware that my wife Cecile had filed for a divorce. I learned of the divorce during the *Cut Zone* broadcast. The filing has pained me and my family deeply. I will admit that, like any couple, we have our challenges. Unfortunately, we do not have the privacy to work out our problems away from the public, especially in these difficult times when I am away a large part of the time representing Folio. It appears my wife was sent the photograph that appeared on the *Cut Zone* broadcast. Cecile was told this was a picture of Shelby Oberman and me. I can confirm that I am not the man in the photograph."

"Then who is the man?" a reporter shouted.

"I would like to finish my statement. But to answer your question, I don't know. Cecile has rescinded the divorce filing and we are entering into couples counseling. My family is important. This has been a difficult time for us. With much soul-searching and a discussion with my family, I have resigned as the CEO of Folio."

My stomach lurched. I turned away from the screen to stare at Ana. Her mouth fell open. She looked as stunned as I felt. "What is he saying?" I said, "He never talked about leaving the company. If anyone would know, it would be me."

Ana shook her head. "I haven't heard a rumor about this. Do you think it's a spur-of-the-moment decision because of the news?"

That was a possibility. But I didn't have a clue without talking to Carter. I looked back at the screen. "What game are you playing?" I mumbled under my breath.

"How long have you and Shelby Oberman been having an affair?" shouted a reporter.

Carter continued to keep calm but engaging for the reporters. I was interested in his answer.

"You guys ask me this all the time." His drawl was thick and folksy. "I love my wife; there's no affair." He punctuated the statement with a grin that said *who are you going to believe, me or your lying eyes?*

The room erupted with reporters calling out questions. I'd heard enough. I'd been publicly dumped. I picked up the remote and turned off the sound from the feed. They recorded the conference, so if there was anything I needed to see, I'd have a tape to review. Carter had taken a sledgehammer to our relationship. Was that what he wanted to talk about last night? Had he planned to fuck me and dump me?

Ana got up. "I'll see what I can find out," she said and rushed out of the office.

I slumped back in my chair. My reputation was ruined. Even if Carter wasn't the man in the photograph, the mention of me in a formal divorce filing as the other woman, from the wife of the powerful man I worked for, gave me a reputation. If I tried to find a job with a top-tier company, I would be seen as a liability. Hell, my days at Folio were probably numbered. I never thought it would end like this. I thought Carter would announce that I was his soulmate and we would be together, everyone be damned. In a day, I'd lost my reputation and the man I loved. Jeeze Louise, I was screwed.

CHAPTER 5

Night Blues

*A*na poked her head into my office. "I just got word the press conference has finished. The team that attended is on their way back to the office."

Carter would be back soon. It might be a little while if he had to tie up some loose ends with the team, then we would talk. I wanted him to tell me this was a sham, that he still loved me and everything would be alright for us.

My nerves were frayed. I was afraid to have another coffee. I pulled up a few files on my laptop and worked until I thought it was close to the time when Carter would call me to his office. I'd just finished running a comb through my hair and freshening my lipstick when Alec drop by my office. "I know you were expecting Carter. He asked me to give you a message. He said he's not coming back to the office. More than likely when he leaves the campus he will be followed; he thinks it's best he return home after the press conference. He will be back in the office tomorrow and you can talk with him then."

"When did Jordan tell you about Carter and me?" I don't know why I asked, but it seemed important to find out who knew about our affair.

He stepped further inside my office and closed the door. "Jordan kept your secret. But remember, I work with the two of you every day. I'd have to be blind not to notice. I asked her once, but she never confirmed my suspicions. I'm on your side, Shelby. Don't worry about me. I was serious when I told Carter that he'll answer to me if he doesn't treat you right."

"I appreciate that. But, do you know what's going on?"

"I don't have the full story either. But you've known him longer than me, so I'm sure you can probably figure it out." He glanced at his watch. "It's been a long day. I should head for home before Jordan starts blowing up my cell phone wondering where I am. Why don't you have dinner with us tonight? I know the kids would love to see Auntie Shelby."

"Thanks, but I think I want to be alone tonight."

I worked in my office until there appeared to be no one on my side of the building. I knew it was late when I heard a vacuum cleaner starting to make a run down the hall. There was nothing at home for me other than a frozen dinner that I was avoiding. I checked my phone. There was nothing from Carter. I tidied my papers. Reaching inside the desk drawer, I pulled out my handbag and set it on top. My jacket was on the coat rack behind me. Standing, I stretched the tiredness out of my body for a few seconds. I plucked my jacket from the hook when I heard someone behind me. "Carter?" I said, making the turn. Sagan Miller stood in the doorway. "How did you get in here?"

"I saw Ana in the lobby. She said you were still in your office. She escorted me upstairs when I told her I wanted to visit you. So here I am."

I slipped on my jacket. "Why exactly are you here?"

He leaned against the doorjamb. "I just left the conference. Some of us had informal time with Carter to discuss the hearings. It ran late. After the day you had, I thought you might need a friend and someone to take you to dinner."

I wasn't in the mood for his banter tonight. I was in the mood for drinking heavily and having a good cry. "As you can see, I'm on my way out."

"I can see that. It's not often I'll pay for a meal. Actually, I'm lying; I'm going to put this on my expense report this month. Have dinner with me," he said as he walked to my desk. "Anything you say tonight will be off the record." He picked up my purse. "Come on, say yes."

I snatched the bag from him. "Give me that; you can't pull off Prada."

CHAPTER 6

Tequila Sunset

"You know, after three shots of tequila you should eat something to soak up the alcohol," he said, studying the three little empty glasses in front of me.

I wasn't drunk enough because I could still see Sagan clearly sitting across from me in a booth sliding a menu toward me. "I'm not hungry." The mariachi music was blaring from the jukebox, and it wasn't helping my headache.

"I guess I'll be the responsible one and order for both of us." He motioned for the waitress to come to our table. I couldn't quite hear what he was saying, but she nodded and left the table.

"What was that all about? I told you I'm not hungry."

"No one's forcing you to eat," he said, watching a couple take a seat next to our booth. "I've ordered sample plates. There might be something you like. I'm betting you will, because they make the best Mexican food in the valley."

When they set two massive plates in front of us, I realized I was starving. I picked up my fork and sampled the chili verde. He was right; it was good. I looked at him and smiled. "Thanks," I said and dug into my plate.

He watched me while I shoveled food into my mouth. "I told you it was good. Are you ready to talk?"

I shook my head. "No," I said and continued to feed myself.

My goal was to get shitfaced, not to eat myself into a better mood. After we finished the meal, I ordered three more tequila shots. I thanked Sagan again for dinner. I told him I'd call a car to get back home. He said he offered me dinner and since he drove to the restaurant, he would drive me home. He pointed out I was in no state to get in the back seat of a car with a driver I didn't know.

"My house is another three blocks on the left," I pointed down the road. He nodded and continued to maneuver the car through the residential street. "Slow down, this is my block."

He pulled the car to the curb a few houses away and switched off the engine. "Is the gray house yours?"

"Yes, why are you stopping here?" I shook my head. I guess he thought the night air would sober me up. It didn't matter, it was close enough to walk. I pushed the button to open the door.

"Wait. I recognize two of the cars in front of your house. They're photographers, freelancers… I've met them. They're trying to catch you and Carter together."

There were cars parked in front of my house I didn't know. He was probably right. "Okay, change of plans," I said, searching inside my purse for my phone. "There's a hotel about three miles away. I'll call them to see if they have an opening. You can drop me off there." Sagan turned the ignition, made a U-turn, then headed for the expressway. "Where are you going? The hotel is in the other direction."

"I know, and I know those reporters. This is a big story. If you land in one of the hotels, someone is bound to notice. Besides, the grainy photograph *Cut Zone* posted, they've also been flashing pictures of you taken at events and your communication director portrait from the company website. Believe me, they know what you look like."

I didn't have family in the state. I had nowhere to crash. I could ask Alec and Jordan or even Ana, but they were employees too, and there was a possibility their houses were targeted as well. We were still driving. "Where are you taking me?"

"I've just invited you to stay at my place." I opened my mouth to say something, but he interrupted me. "I've got a spare room and, other than the place needs a little attention from a maid service, it's actually pretty nice. I'm not part of Folio. We have no connection. You'd be safe with me. You can stay until you find another place."

I was feeling the effects of the last three tequila shots. I held onto Sagan for support, staggering with him to his front door. He propped me up next to the door with one hand. His other hand tried to put the key in the lock. He pushed the key in but his hold on me wasn't as firm and I almost slipped to the ground before he caught me. Our noses were almost touching. I put my arms around his neck. He was staring at me and I was looking back at him. God, he was hot. So-freaking-hot. I loved men with black hair and blue eyes. He was exactly my type, a few years older. Big, muscled form like a swimmer. I know I was wet. I giggled. Carter was right; I was a dirty girl and a drunk one too. He looked like he would kiss me or maybe I would kiss him.

His face wasn't in focus, and I didn't feel well. I pushed past him into the house. "What's wrong? Let me help you inside. You can collapse on the couch."

Dishes in the sink and pizza boxes on the dining room table, the place didn't need a little attention from a maid, it needed a hazmat crew to clean. "Where is the guest room?" Maybe if I laid down. I belched. He pointed. I made my way into the room with Sagan close behind me. My stomach... "Bathroom, I need the bathroom." He pointed to a door in the room. I burst through in time and fell to my knees, gripping the toilet and wretched the chili verde, tequila, salsa, and chips into the porcelain throne.

"Are you alright?" he said, leaning against the sink.

I lifted my face from the bowl. "I've been better." I turned back and vomited again.

He switched on the water, grabbed a washcloth, and held it under the water. "Are you finished?"

I lifted my head. "I think that about does it."

He held out his hand. I got to my feet and took the warm cloth he offered. "You'll feel better if you wash your face. There's mouthwash underneath the sink in case you want to get rid of the taste of your dinner." I did what he instructed. "Do you think you're steady enough to walk to the bed on your own?" I gave him a look that said please, I'm not an invalid, and got to the bed. "Wait here, I'll be right back." I laid back contemplating the ceiling, hoping the room wouldn't spin, then I'd be in deeper shit. He returned with two sports bottles. He offered me one. "Drink this," he said, taking a place beside me on the bed.

I sat up. "What's this?"

"It's mostly water with some orange juice mixed in for flavor. It's easier to drink it down that way."

I took the offered bottle, while he set the other on the side table. "Why do I have to drink this?" I asked.

"Drinking alcohol dehydrates you." He settled on his side, watching me. "You vomited everything else that was in your stomach. More dehydration. If you don't want to have a hangover, then drink these two sports bottles filled with my water orange juice mixture and you won't have a hangover. You might feel a little tired from the effects of your drinking, but you won't have a hangover."

I think he was right, and I wasn't going to argue. I couldn't be hung over at work tomorrow. Carter promised to speak with me and I had to be sober for our discussion. Sagan dutifully watched me suck down the contents of one sports bottle. I told him I needed a little more time before I'd begin the second. I was feeling better and looked around at the room. As guest rooms go, it was unremarkable, clean, and untouched by the chaos from the other rooms.

"There're clothes in the closet; use what you need." Sagan's big hand pushed at the small of my back, launching me off the bed. I opened the door. His clothes and assorted female clothing were in the closet. I pulled out a pink shirt. "Have you been exploring your feminine side?" He leaned forward to look around me.

"Not lately, but that's not my stuff. It's my sister's." His grin wasn't convincing.

"Ah huh, sister. Then why are there different sizes?"

"Oh yeah, I forgot sometimes my cousins stay with me too." He looked like a healthy male adult. Not sure why it surprised me.

He moved off the bed. "I know you're tired. I'll let you get some sleep. Unless there's another way I can be of service?" There was no mistaking what he was suggesting.

"Thanks for your help. If I think of something, I'll let you know."

He shrugged. "Remember to finish the second bottle." He left the room.

It wasn't that late. I picked up my phone to check messages. There was nothing from Carter. I needed clothes and other things. There was nothing appropriate in Sagan's closet to wear to Folio. Forget about doing the walk of shame in the same clothes I wore yesterday. After the press conference, it was important I look unaffected by the scandal. I sent a text to my stylist Mia, who worked for the clothing service I used. We had been working together to style my wardrobe for a few years. She was overjoyed when I asked her to purchase everything from suits, casual wear, pajamas, toiletries, and make-up. She promised to have work clothes and essentials delivered in the morning before I left for work.

A text zipped in. It was from Carter. "Sorry, I know this is difficult. I wish you were here with me now. I love you... C"

I smiled. Wearing something new tomorrow would be perfect. Glad I made the call to Mia. I wanted to look drop dead gorgeous when I heard Carter's brilliant plan.

CHAPTER 7

Eugene

Sunshine flooded the room. I was half asleep, on my stomach, thinking I might ask Sagan to put up heavier curtains to block out some of this irritating cheery light, when I felt hot breath and a tongue lick the back of my neck. Was Sagan in bed with me? I rolled over and scrambled to the edge of the bed furthest away from him. Damn it, there was a dog in my bed. No, that wasn't right. He was large enough to be a small pony. "Sagan?" I shouted, not taking my eyes off the dog. "Where are you? Get in here now!" The dog cocked his head. I blinked. He didn't look like he wanted me to be his chew toy, but I couldn't be sure. My host appeared in the doorway in pajama bottoms. I almost caught my breath looking at his bare chest. He folded his arms and leaned against the doorjamb.

"Eugene, what did I tell you about bothering the guests before you've been properly introduced?" The dog lowered his head. "Come on, boy, give her some room." He bounced off the bed, standing next to him. "I'm sorry, he likes to stay in this room. How did you sleep?"

"His name is Eugene?"

"He's a boy. What's the problem?"

"Nothing." I looked over at the dog. I guess he looked like a Eugene. "He's big."

"Eugene's not that big; he's a Bull Mastiff."

"Fine. My sleep was fine."

"How's your head?"

That's right, I'd been doing tequila shots last night. I was tired, but there was no hangover. "You should sell that cure."

"Sell it? It's common sense." He laughed. "I put coffee on and there're waffles and blueberries if you're hungry. Orange juice, of course."

I was wearing one of his oversized shirts, but I just noticed that it felt wet. I glanced down at my front; I must have gotten drool on it. I groaned. Sagan and Eugene both gave me a pitying look. "You can wear whatever is in the closet or the dresser. I'll see you in the kitchen. Before I forget, there's a package for you. A woman came by earlier and dropped it off."

I searched through the closet and the drawers again for clothes. I rummaged through the box Mia left. She packed the box with work clothes. No casual wear or pajamas. I assumed that would come later today. I found a T-shirt and a pair of shorts that were at least a size too small in the closet and put them on.

Eugene was in the living room working on a real chew toy when I passed through. Sagan was busy moving about the kitchen when he looked over at me. His eyes grew to the size of two large disks when he saw me. He was looking at me like I was a pork chop. I guess my clothes were a little too provocative. He tore his gaze away from my chest, turned and picked up two plates. I slipped onto a stool at the counter, as he placed breakfast in front of me. I thought we would have a toaster pastry. But no, I spied the waffle batter, waffle iron, and a basket of blueberries. I also noticed a pitcher of orange juice, butter, and real maple syrup. "Are you secretly a chef? I mean, this is a lot for a weekday just before work."

"Cooking is a hobby." He popped a blueberry in his mouth. "I don't normally cook like this when I'm by myself, but you're here and I wanted you to feel welcome. I have pecans, if you want to have those on your waffles too."

There's nothing hotter than a guy cooking you a meal in the kitchen. He was still in his pajama bottoms but had found a T-shirt to put on. I'm glad I didn't know this about him the few times I met him for coffee. I might've jumped his bones right then. I forked off a portion of the light, fluffy waffle with blueberries, wiping it up with butter and syrup. "This is good."

He put down his orange juice. "Glad you like it. Are you ready to talk?"

"No," I said, and I continued to stuff my face full of waffles.

I helped him clean up after our meal. It was fun spending time with him in the kitchen like we were a real couple. He was so handsome as we chatted, stopping briefly to tell me where to put a dish away. "I've got to leave for an early appointment." he said. "You'll be here on your own. I've left a key to the house and also a key to my car. You can use it while you're staying here. If the press is following you, there's a good chance they know what you normally drive. I'll catch a ride or rent a car. It's no problem. I'll stay longer if you need me for anything. Like help in the shower?"

I rolled my eyes. He was right; I didn't protest. "Thank you, I'd like to repay you for any expenses you incur on my account. Really, I won't take no for an answer."

"Fair enough, but did I mention that I have a generous expense account?"

I laughed. "Really, I'm serious, I want to pay you back."

He placed the drying cloth on a hook. "If you need me for something, anything, let me know. This can't be easy for you."

I shook my head. "Thanks, I'll be okay. This is one of Carter's big schemes."

Sagan

Southbound traffic moved at a sluggish pace this morning. Thank God I had a reverse commute, or I'd be inching along like an earthworm in that northbound parking lot.

I punched through my playlist and found nothing that fit my mood. Shelby telling me that everything would be alright had me worried. She was probably right. Carter could wiggle out of anything. He was the master of win/win.

My mind was going over the events of last night and how it could have gone another way when a call came through on the car console. I swore when I recognized the number and pushed the receive button. "I wondered when you'd be calling," I said, irritated. "What the hell, Carter, why didn't you tell me you were together? I asked you if there was something between you and Shelby. You told me no. You even encouraged me to pursue her."

"Do I need to remind you that you're a reporter?"

"I thought we were beyond that, or is that a lie as well?"

"You need to see the bigger picture. If this was about me and someone else, I would have told you, but, like me, you want to protect Shelby."

"What do you want?"

"I called to thank you for helping her out last night. I knew she had nowhere to go and you're the best person to take care of her right now. I've got a lot of loose ends to tie up before I leave the company, but I plan to talk with Shelby later today. I don't know if she'll agree to what I'll propose. Either way, you might need to help her out a little longer. I know you're irritated with me, but you like her. Don't pretend you're not enjoying this time with her."

Like Shelby? That was an understatement. If I was honest with myself, I'd admit I was in love with her. She occupied my thoughts more than she should, and it didn't help when she appeared in all of my dirty fantasies.

I'd been talking to her for the last five years and I couldn't get any further than meeting her a few times for coffee. For a while I thought there might be more, but she abruptly cut it off. Last night when I thought she would kiss me, I was about to sweep her up and take her to my bed. But she was too sick and vulnerable from Carter's antics to know what she wanted. I won't take advantage of her; she has to come to me. I was surprised when Carter suggested I take her to dinner. Even more surprised when Shelby said yes. "You're welcome," I said. "I like her, but it's always been one-sided."

"That's not what I've seen. She stares at you like you might be the second coming when you're not looking." Without seeing Carter's face, I couldn't tell if he was telling the truth.

"But if she's not interested..." He left the statement hanging.

That was a kick in my gut. Maybe that's why I lashed out with the same old argument. "After all these years, why haven't you told her the truth? She has a right to know."

"Why haven't you?"

That was a good question. Why was I holier than Carter?

"Look, truth is relative, and I don't think it's that important. It changes nothing."

He brushed it off too lightly again. But I know this is important. Why couldn't he see the damage it would bring? "Think again," I said. "If you don't tell her, I will."

"That might be a mistake, but I'll leave it to you. My advice is, don't cherry-pick the truth. You'll need to tell it all."

CHAPTER 8

Number Three

Carter was in the building. His new secretary, Regina, let me know I had an appointment scheduled with him at the end of the day. He had a lot of work to do before he resigned his position. He would announce it formally to the company in an all-hands meeting on Friday. Brian Westfield would be the new CEO. I liked Brian; he was a solid administrator and would be a good CEO, but he was not fuckable.

It was about 6 o'clock when I arrived at Carter's office. Regina was still at her desk. She'd been his secretary for only about four months. She was in her early 20s and the complete opposite of me. I had dark hair and eyes; she was blonde and blue-eyed. She had porcelain skin and mine was the color of honey. Carter had a favorite body type. We were both busty, tall, slender, and leggy. We never liked each other. I knew this immediately when I saw her talking to Carter. It was obvious she was in love with him and saw me as competition.

Carter was sitting at his desk on the phone. He motioned me to the chair when I entered. "No, the formal statement or announcement will be done Friday at the all-hands meeting," he said. "It's just a formality but I want to talk to them. No problem, we'll talk more tomorrow." He hung up the phone, distracted.

It was the end of the day and this was casual Carter I was looking at. Sleeves rolled up, collar opened at the neck, hair a bit disheveled. "Why don't we go into the compartment?" he said. "We'll be more comfortable." He picked up the phone. "Regina, you can go home now; Shelby is my last meeting. We'll be gone from here in about an hour. Thank you, have a good evening."

We got to our feet. Carter motioned toward the entrance behind the panel. "I've poured wine; we can sit and talk. I know you have a lot of questions." Carter was close behind me as I moved to open the door to the compartment. This was a spacious two-bedroom apartment with a view to the city. We travelled through the foyer, kitchen, and into the living room. Two glasses of wine sat on a sideboard. He caught my hand and pulled me to him, kissing me while his fingers played in my hair. I held onto him; his cock was already semi-hard through the fabric. He broke off. "I've wanted to kiss you for the longest time." His sigh was deep.

And all I wanted to do was reverse time before the hearings. My hands were on his chest, the warm muscles underneath my palms. My fingers began to unbutton him, an automatic habit I performed when we were alone. He caught my hands. "No, I'll have you under me in the bedroom if you keep this up. I'm too horny; you'd have it a bit rough."

I kissed his chest. "Still want to fuck me all night?"

He ran his hand over my behind. "Always. God, I love to watch you. The look in your eyes when you come."

"Do you still love me, Carter? Have I lost you?" I hadn't planned to ask. I know I sounded desperate, but he knew how much I needed him.

He pulled me back into his embrace, his face in my hair. "No, never. Nothing has changed between us. I said those things to protect you."

"Then if it was only words, let's just—"

"There's more, Shelby. We have to talk. Let me get your glass."

He picked up the two glasses and handed me one. "To changes," he said.

I sipped but didn't return his toast. "What's happening?"

He frowned. "I'm leaving the company; you know Brian takes over as the new CEO."

"Why did you decide to leave without telling me first?"

"There was no time. Events were moving too fast. Your boss's wife naming you in a divorce action would ruin your career, among other things. The only way I could protect you was to deny the affair and leave."

"I get that. She wanted to hurt you by destroying me, two for one."

"There's something else. California is a no-fault state. She doesn't need to provide evidence of infidelity for a judge to grant her a divorce. We have children under twenty-one and assets. She wanted to prevent me from giving any assets to you before the divorce was final."

Now I understood; we couldn't have a relationship until the marriage ended. I didn't know how much Carter was worth, but with his company, I'm sure the two had built up considerable assets. It might take time to come to an agreement. No, that wasn't right. "But you said Cecile rescinded the divorce, and you were going into couples counseling; did I hear that correctly?"

He took my hand and led me to the couch. "I've been going over this in my head a million times and none of the scenarios I've looked at will make this any easier." I sat, not wanting to hear his explanation. I felt like a child sitting there waiting for the parent to give me bad news. Telling me I had to be brave. The knot in my gut told me everything was about to change. "Yes, I'm back with Cecile, but I never left her. This pains me. I love you, I truly love you, Shelby, but what we have is over."

I wanted to dissolve into nothing. He was talking, but I couldn't concentrate on his words.

"The truth is, I'm in love with two women. I didn't deserve either of you. Cecile knew about you and tolerated our relationship because she loved me. She gave me children and stood by me. You gave me the best years of your life. I was selfish with both of you. I should've made a choice, but I couldn't and in the end I didn't."

"Until Cecile ended it for you. If you love me, just pay her the money."

He sat back, looking around the room. "I wish I'd known you when I was younger. If we were both about the same age. We could've explored life together. But because you're with me you're missing out."

His old fears were cropping up again. "Is this about the age difference? I told you, Carter, it means nothing. I want you."

"I know you want to have children. I don't want to start another family."

"It doesn't matter. I don't want kids."

"Shelby, you're not a very good liar. You dote over every child an employee brings into the building. You try to spend as much time as you can with Jordan's kids. You need your own."

"We can have a baby," I suggested. "We could get married."

"No!"

It stunned me. We never had this conversation, but I thought surely, we might have a child together. That he would leave Cecile and we would marry.

"Shelby, I don't want to marry you. I'm sorry but that's the truth."

"What was this? You just wanted to use me for ten years?"

"I fell in love with you the first time I met you. I've been faithful to Cecile our whole marriage until you came to the company. You were young. I thought you would get bored and eventually leave me.

But you never did. I tried to end it several times. I'm an imperfect man, Shelby; I couldn't leave you."

"Imperfect man?" I got up and placed my drink on the end table. It was time to leave. "An imperfect man is someone who drinks a little too much on Saturday night. You, Carter, are foursquare in asshole territory."

"You're angry. I'm sorry, but I can't change this. Cecile has already left for Montreal. She wants us to live where she grew up. She still has family there. I'll follow her in a few days after I tie up things here."

I'd seen this look in meetings before. There was no leeway. He had decided. He couldn't have loved me. I know it felt like love for me. "You can leave, Carter, but I'll follow you. I'll stay close until you come back to me."

"No, you won't." The tiredness returned to his face. "Even if you came to the city, I won't see you. This has to be the end."

My tears were bottled up, I was so angry. I couldn't sort out if the anger was from him dumping me or that I was so stupid not to see this coming. He had to see that I loved him more than Cecile. Would do anything for him. I was staring at the unapproachable Carter. He stood, ready to walk me out. "Then if this is truly over," I said. "I want to be with you one last time. Your birthday is in two days. Cecile is gone; we can celebrate it together."

Carter shook his head and looked away. "What's this, a honey trap? Do you think if we sleep together that I'll change my mind?"

"I'm thinking I want to be with the man I love one last time. And I want to make him happy on his birthday. I know we can't go anywhere in public after that announcement you made to the press. But we can celebrate here in the compartment. I asked you to send me your birthday list. You still haven't done it. Fine, part of our deal is I only need to choose one of the items on your list. And I choose number three."

To say there was a war going on behind his eyes would be an understatement. Seeing surprise, lust, and wanting all rolled into one was almost laughable. "I can't–."

I cut off his protest. "Think about it, Carter, I know your dick will. You've been asking me to do a threesome for the last five years and you're going to pass that up? If I remember the listing, you said it would be up to you to choose the third person. My God, you've been trying to get me prepped for this for years. You know how I feel. I told you I didn't want to, that allowing another woman in our bed was the limit. I've done everything else you've asked. Every dirty, nasty fantasy except for this. What was your logic for me to go along? That 'all cats look grey in the dark.' Or my favorite, 'When you're in a sexual fever, it doesn't matter who's touching you.'" I did a Carter imitation using that Tennessee twang, "'I want to watch you make love, baby, I want to watch you come.'"

He caught me by the shoulders. "Stop it Shelby, this isn't you."

"The hell it is." I pushed his hands away. "You know Cecile will never give you this and I will. I'll be here in two days waiting for you at 8 o'clock. And you will stay with me the whole night." I headed towards the door. "I almost forgot. Part of the listing says you will choose my outfit. Make sure it's somewhere in the bedroom before I get here."

"I won't be here, Shelby," Carter called after me.

I turned. "Oh, I think you will. You'd never miss the best fuck of your life."

CHAPTER 9

Numb

I drove around the city for a while. The faint scent of Sagan's aftershave reminded me I was driving his car. I wasn't ready to go back to his place. I didn't want to face him and I sure as hell didn't want to talk about my meeting with Carter.

What was I thinking, offering him a night he'd never forget as my revenge? I pulled the car over to the side of the road. I was in Main Street Cupertino, watching people strolling through the area, slipping into restaurants, meeting friends for dinner. Maybe this wasn't such a great idea. Carter made me so freaking mad, sex was the only thing I could use to lash out at him. I knew him. I knew him so well. He would not pass this up.

"Shelby," I said to myself, "woman up. Do what you promised; walk away and never look back... Then miss him for the rest your life." I crossed my arms on the steering wheel, leaned my head against them, and cried.

I hoped Sagan would be out when I arrived, but the scent of garlic drifting from the kitchen, soft music, and pots banging told me he was in. The hazmat crew must have visited while I was gone. The place was spotless. I headed for my room, treading softly, but I would have to pass the kitchen and I wasn't in a mood to face him. I reached the kitchen. Sagan was bent at the waist, two enormous oven mitts covering his hands, pulling out a pan from the oven. The counter was set for dinner, a carafe of wine and two glasses sitting out. It looked achingly homey. A handsome guy in a waist apron waiting for me to come back home, after the day I had... it made me want to cry again. I stayed too long in the doorway watching him. He caught sight of me, a smile drifting across his face. "You're here. I'd hoped you'd be home soon. I wasn't sure. How was your day? Did everything go okay?"

He asked about my day. Who does that? "Work was fine, other things could have been better..."

"Want to talk?"

"No." I passed by him and headed for the guest room. He followed.

"I made dinner. I thought we could..."

I threw my jacket on the chair and kicked off my heels. Mia had dropped off another package. It was sitting in the corner. This one had to contain some casual wear. "That sounds good, but I'm not hungry." Maybe he would get the hint that I wanted to be alone.

He lingered in the doorway. "I was hoping for more than Eugene's company. I won't even have that; he's at a sleepover."

"Dogs have sleepovers?"

"Eugene is very popular. His BFF is a standard French Poodle two doors down." He stepped inside the room and took my hand. "Come on, I've been slaving over a hot stove; you've at least got to taste it." He pulled me along before I could protest, set me on a stool, poured a glass of wine, and moved it in my direction. Picking up a wooden spoon, he scooped a little from the dish and held it to my lips. "Here, have a taste."

I dutifully ate. "That's really good; what is it?" I wasn't much of a cook, but I was a whiz with the microwave.

"It's something I put together. It's a casserole, kind of. Sample the wine."

I drank. "Yummy too." I started to push off the stool.

"Don't leave," he said with concern in his eyes. "I'm guessing you talked to Carter and it didn't go well." It came out in a rush.

"I don't want to talk about it." I got to my feet. "I'm sorry that you cooked on my account, but I've had a rough day..."

He raked frustrated fingers through his hair. "Look, what you tell me is off the record. In fact, everything is off the record until you say it isn't, so talk to me. You've got to talk to someone."

"I can't." It came out as a frustrated moan. What part of 'I can't' did he not understand?

He exhaled. "I'm not a bad person, Shelby. I want to help if I can. Whatever you need. Let me help you." He moved closer, gathering me in his arms. His big body surrounded me. I wanted to rage – there were so many emotions that needed to get out – but he kept me tight to his body. I held onto him, needing the closeness. Carter had rejected me; hollow didn't begin to cover how unloved I felt. Sagan's hand stroked my hair. "You're so beautiful. He's a fool not to keep you," he murmured into my hair.

I wanted to get back to my house and grieve alone. I'd been waiting forever for Carter to make this right. After holding it together these last days, I was tired and crashing. "Help me," I sobbed into his chest. "Take this goddamn pain away, before I die from it." I looked up at him. "I don't want to hurt anymore." He squeezed me then kissed me on the forehead. His fingers were in my hair, tightening his grip, pulling my head back. His lips were demanding, kiss consuming, and I held on, gasping for air. He walked me backwards toward my room. We stopped when my back hit the wall. I was tugging at his T-shirt, trying to get it off. He pushed my hands away to pull free of his shirt and yanked mine over my head. I was kissing him, tongue probing, needing to taste him. His hand was searching underneath my skirt, the fabric inching up along my hip, his fingers under the lace of my panties, slipping them down. His fingers were playing with me, opening me.

"You're so wet," came the hoarse whisper. "You want this." I fumbled for his cock, his bulge hard underneath his jeans. "Unzip me and take me out," he said.

My fingers found his cock, hard and erect. I stroked its thick length. I was sliding down, dropping to my knees, wanting badly to suck him, but his strong hands held me up. His body pinned me to the wall, unfastening my skirt, the fabric falling to the floor. His fingers were playing with my clit, my pussy aching for him to be inside me. He moaned in my ear when my hand stroked his cock. He kissed me again hard, not giving me time. His hands rubbed my hips, slipping under my thighs, pulling me up, my legs wrapped around his hips. "Remember you wanted this."

"I need it," I whispered.

His cock rammed into me; my back slammed against the wall. I gasped, accepting him inside me. My arms around his neck, I held on tight, my back meeting the wall with each hard thrust. "I want more," I whispered. "Use me." His fingers dug into my flesh, muscles flexing, keeping me in place. His face at my neck breathing me in, grunting with the effort to keep me where he needed me, until he was done. I came first, my body spent. He followed a few thrusts later. He released me, and I sank to the floor.

Sagan towered over me, uncertain. I looked past him to the kitchen. Everything ordinary and unchanged. Our meal untouched on the counter. He held out his hand. I couldn't look at him. I gathered my clothes and scrambled to my feet. "I need to be alone," I mumbled. I walked to my room and closed the door.

CHAPTER 10

Sapphires

I walked out of my room the next morning ready to apologize to Sagan, but he was gone. I found a note on the kitchen counter next to orange juice and chocolate muffins. *Shelby, Eugene and I are staying with a friend. I'm giving you space if that's what you want. I'll come back if you need me. Call me anytime. I'll come. Sagan.*

I sat in my office staring at a coffee mug, thinking about the note Sagan left and how pathetic my life was right now. I was too much of a coward to call Sagan and apologize. There would be time enough to talk after Carter was gone. I'd spend tonight alone at Sagan's using the time to prepare for tomorrow's events and the gift I promised to give Carter for his birthday.

It was Friday, Carter's last day with the company and his birthday. The all-hands meeting was live-streamed to all Folio facilities across the US and around the world. It was a mixture of his good-bye to a company he founded and built and a birthday celebration. I endured it all with a smile, apprehensive that later we would be together in a kinky threesome sex romp.

Regina walked into my office with a you-are-such-a-loser-smirk on her face to deliver an envelope from Carter. I didn't care what that witch thought of me, Carter would be gone soon and this made-up competition in her head would be over.

Shelby, you don't have to do this. But if you're determined, and I know how stubborn you can be once you get something into your head, you need to know I can't get to the compartment until 8:30. We can spend as much time as you like together, but it won't change my mind. Carter

I knew one night with Carter wouldn't fix everything. He'd been a big part of my life for the last ten years. He was the only man I'd ever been with, except for that quickie with Sagan. I needed time to get used to the idea that Carter wouldn't be in my life anymore.

I arrived at Carter's office at 7 p.m., pulling my overnight bag behind me. Regina was not at her desk. I couldn't figure out if she was gone for the day or if she had just stepped away. Carter and I were the only people who had access to his office. I swiped my badge, entered, and quickly moved behind the panel. I traveled through the foyer, kitchen, and stopped in the living room. The night was clear with a pale moon and stars with the twinkling city below. Many nights we had sat here enjoying the view while making love.

I walked into the master bedroom and flipped on the light. A dress and a pair of stilettos were arranged on the bed. No panties or bra. I picked up the dress. A long drapey fabric in midnight blue, Carter's favorite color. The Grecian style, with a single seam down the front, would cling to my body. The low neckline would enhance my breasts, and the slits on both sides of the dress would reveal long lengths of my legs. I wondered if the other woman would be dressed in something as elegant or if Carter would prefer to dress her in something slutty. I didn't have time to worry about that. I needed to shower and dress. I pulled out my phone and called up a playlist. The music rose around me from the synced-up speakers. I needed to relax. I pulled off my shirt and noticed a note on the dresser. *Shelby, please wear your hair up tonight and what is contained in these boxes. This is my gift to you. Carter.* This was the second note I'd received from him today and neither was signed with love. It hurt, a lot.

Three boxes sat next to the note. I opened the first and largest box. A white gold necklace studded with diamonds and sapphires spread out in a triangle pattern. In the second box sat a cuff bracelet, also diamonds and sapphires. The third contained matching earrings. They were gorgeous, expensive, and probably one of a kind.

I spent more time than usual dressing. It was important I exceed Carter's expectations tonight. Once I fastened the last piece of jewelry, there was a knock, and the front door opened. "Shelby?" Carter called from the living room. "Sorry, I'm running a little late." The playlist had hit a love song from the early 90s. I checked the mirror one last time. I walked into the living room. Carter was there in a custom suit, looking like male perfection. He leaned back against the wall and gave me a long, appreciative look. "I don't think I've ever seen you looking so exquisite." My heart quivered and for a moment; I'd forgotten this would be our last time together.

"Thank you. You look very handsome, Mr. Morrison." I had to play my part. I threw the party, but it would be Carter calling the shots tonight. He would direct the play.

He went to the drinks cupboard and brought out a bucket of champagne. The pop from the cork felt like a celebration. He handed me a glass. Looking into my eyes, he ran his hand slowly down my arm. I stared back at him, suppressing an urge to mew at his touch. "To you, my beauty." I smiled, and we touched glasses.

I held up my glass. "Happy birthday. May it be everything you want and more."

Carter's mouth quirked up. It suddenly became awkward, but we still touched glasses. How could it be happy if I was forcing him to be here with me?

"I haven't heard this song in a long time." He recovered nicely. "This must be from that playlist you made from me a few years ago."

He held out his hand. "Will you dance with me, Ms. Oberman?" It was like Beauty and the Beast. I didn't care. I put my arms around his neck and we swayed to the music. I gazed into his eyes, his desire burning. I almost stopped the dance, wanting to lead him to the bedroom, until he kissed me sweet and slow like the kisses we shared when we first met. I didn't want to ruin the moment, I just wanted to stay in his arms.

Soft knocking on the door broke the moment. Carter turned his head to the sound, stopping the dance. "Our guest is here." There was no mistaking his excitement. "Why don't you wait in the bedroom and I'll call you when we're ready."

I nodded and left.

Too nervous to sit, I stayed near the door, straining to hear. He was talking to a woman. He said something too low for me to understand. She laughed, warm and sensual. It was Regina, his secretary. I sank onto the bed, hurt that he would choose her, but I wasn't surprised. This would be awful. Sex with a woman I didn't like. Regina hated me and used every meeting I had with her to drive that point home.

"Shelby," Carter called, "Join us, we're ready."

I took a deep breath, faked a smile, and returned to the living room. The music was drifting softly when I entered. Carter stood at the window, sipping champagne, looking out at the view. Sagan Miller rose from his chair, dressed in a trendy suit, expertly tailored to fit. Carter turned around in time to watch the reunion. Sagan's lopsided grin regarded me. "You look gorgeous tonight. Are you excited?"

I looked at Carter. "Where is Regina?" Did three just turn into four? Carter and I stared at each other. Sagan looked at us, bewildered.

"Regina is gone," Carter said. "She stayed long enough to escort Sagan in the elevator to the office. I'm not sure I know what you mean; he's my third," he said, putting his glass down on the table.

"This is not what we agreed to and you know it. Why is Sagan here?"

"He said you invited me to dinner to celebrate his birthday," Sagan offered. "Is there a problem?"

"You always have to have the last word, don't you?" I said, looking at a smug Carter. "You always have to manipulate everything."

"I thought this was a better solution." His casual response was maddening.

"What's this?" I asked. "Are you bi or just curious?" Carter's face grew dark. That got him; I'd struck a nerve.

"I don't understand," Sagan said. "Is this some bizarre game you're playing?"

Carter and I both threw him a stare to shut up. Sagan sank back in his chair and waited.

"Don't worry, this will be ironed out directly," Carter said.

"My gift to you was genuine," I said. "So now we play this to the end. Sagan," I called to him, still looking at Carter, "do you like me?"

"What's this about?" Sagan asked, still no clue.

"Answer the question."

"Yes?"

"Enough to fuck me in front of Carter?"

Sagan didn't answer. I turned to him. "Will you fuck me while Carter watches?"

"What's this about?" He glanced at Carter.

I walked to the drinks cupboard, poured myself a champagne, and drank deeply. "I think our guest deserves an explanation," I said, raising my glass to Carter. Would you like me to fill him in on our little game?"

"I want you and Sagan to go to dinner," Carter hurried through his explanation. "I've made reservations at your favorite restaurant. Let's end this now. Start a new life, Shelby."

"Carter, you can't just give me to somebody. Who does that? It doesn't work that way." He walked away from me to take a seat at the couch.

"Sagan," I said, "Carter and I've been together for a long time. We discovered early on we were crap at buying presents for each other. So, we invented the list. It was like a gift registry, but with only three items. The buyer can give all three but no less than one item from the list, and you can't list the same item for all three slots. It was a handy little guide for our birthdays and holidays. But you know how things evolve. We started with something easy like socks and flowers, but then it turned interesting. Anyway, six years ago Carter put a threesome on his list and lobbied hard for the gift. I never gave him that present. Tonight, for his birthday, I agreed to the threesome. Rules say he picks the third and directs the play. I thought his third would be Regina."

Sagan looked at Carter. "Is that why you asked me here?"

"No," Carter responded, annoyed. "It was just dinner. I want Shelby to move on. I thought you could help."

Sagan crossed his arms, glaring at Carter. "You need to tell her."

"It has nothing to do with this. Why don't you go into the other room and let me talk to Shelby?"

"Nope, he stays." I said, and took another sip of my drink.

"You know you never wanted to do this. You're trying to change my mind with this stunt. Face it, you weren't really going to go through with it."

I leaned against the cupboard. "It's Carter's fantasy to have two or more pairs of bouncy boobs in his bed."

"That's enough, Shelby, you're embarrassing yourself."

"No, love, I'm embarrassing you."

Carter folded his arms, talking to Sagan. "Shelby would have you believe that she doesn't want a threesome, and that she was doing this only to please me. If I wanted to hurt her, I could have asked Regina, but the two women hate each other. Shelby doesn't like

Regina because she's female. Five years ago, and every year since then, Ms. Oberman has listed a threesome on her list."

"Okay, Carter, you win." I put my glass down.

"You see," Carter continued with unmistakable glee, "she likes dueling cocks. And the kicker is, the threesome appeared on her list five years ago when you came into town. What's that; crickets I hear? Believe me, she's wet just thinking about having the both of us."

Sagan got to his feet. "I'll take you home, if that's what you want."

Sagan made a silent plea for me to leave with him. Carter walked over to stand near him, not happy this didn't go as he planned. I move to them, the three of us in a close circle. I put my arms around Sagan's neck, pulling him in for a kiss. Carter didn't move; he watched Sagan's hesitation to respond, but I held him until he returned my kiss, his hands running down my sides, pulling me to him. Carter stepped away. I flung a hand out to catch his arm, stopping him. Sagan still holding me, I twisted to Carter for a kiss. His hands slid over my breasts while Sagan squeezed my ass. For a few moments we were three, and the promise of what this could become was real. Sagan's hands fell from me. He stepped away, rubbing his face. "We can still have a three," I whispered to Carter. Carter glanced at Sagan, who paced near the chair.

I knew Carter wanted us together; he was as turned on as I was. He wasn't lying when he said I wanted two men. Torment replaced Sagan's cocky grin; he avoided looking at either of us.

I moved to Sagan, taking his hand. "Say yes," I pleaded with him, trying to get him to look at me. I wanted this more than I could have imagined. I squeezed his hand. "I want you too. Please say yes," I whispered, keeping my gaze on him, but he was studying our entwined fingers. "Tell him it's okay, Carter," I said, not taking my gaze from Sagan, "that it's just sex. It stays here, it's for one night only."

"She's right, the movers are coming in late afternoon tomorrow. You can join us, or not. It's your choice." Sagan's attention came back to Carter, and something unreadable passed between them. Carter maneuvered around me to stand in front of an uncertain Sagan and placed his hands on his shoulders. "I want you to understand," Carter said, "what we do here changes nothing between us. I love you. I love you, no matter what you decide."

Sagan slipped out of his grip and sank into the chair. "You can't mean that, not after all this time, not after everything that's happened."

Carter looked down at him. Sagan scooted forward, body hunched, face in hands. He didn't respond to the declaration. Were we in love with the same man?

"What's going on?" I demanded, shocked at Carter's statement. "Are you already lovers?" Neither would answer, still frozen in place by the moment. My stomach twisted that there was something else about Carter that I didn't know. I shook Carter's arm. "Say something, God damn it."

Carter snapped out of his stupor, recognition returning to his eyes as he focused on me. He moved to my back, his arms around me, kissing my hair. "I'm sorry, Shelby, I know what this must look like, but it's nothing like that. Sagan is my son."

Sagan tilted his attention up to me but said nothing.

Carter turned me to face him. "I was a teenager when he was born. His mother raised him. I wasn't allowed to see him, but I managed it a few times. I reached out to Sagan when he turned eighteen, but he wasn't ready to meet me. We met when he came to the valley. We're working out a lot of shit together. I'm not going to lie; this will be one more thing on the pile."

Sagan looked less troubled, but there was still something left unsaid. I never would have guessed a father and son. God help me, I was dirty; I wanted this, them, even more.

Carter brushed my shoulder. "He's been asking about you ever since you met at one of your industry meetings. He wanted to know if there was anything between us. I denied the affair to protect you. I told him to pursue you, even helped him a few times. This can't be easy for him. I think he's in love with you."

Looking at the two of them, I could see the resemblance. They were both big men, same lean-muscled body. Sagan had some of his mother's looks, eyes not as blue; he wasn't a carbon copy. Carter might have looked like this when he was younger.

I went to Sagan, his eyes regarding me when I sat on his lap. "You asked me to talk to you," I said.

"You picked an interesting time for a chat."

Carter must have given up on dinner. He discarded his jacket and tie, placing them on the couch, then headed for the drinks cabinet.

"I've been known to have great timing, when it's important," I said. "What Carter said about me is true. You're the reason I put that threesome on my list."

He didn't appear to be surprised by the confession, just rested a hand on my back. "I stopped having coffee with you because I was afraid I would be unfaithful to Carter. Which is ridiculous, but that's another conversation."

Sagan stared at my cleavage as I spoke; the point of the necklace tear-dropped between my breasts. "Your necklace; it's unusual the way the gems catch the light when you move."

I ran my fingers from the hollow of my neck, stopping at the teardrop. His eyes followed my fingers. "Thank you, it was a gift from Carter."

"Here," Carter said, interrupting. "This is the gin you like." He handed Sagan a glass. "It looks like we're going to be here for a while; I suggest you get comfortable."

Sagan took the drink, almost draining the clear liquid from the glass. Carter retreated to the couch, stretched out, savored his champagne, and watched this play out.

I removed the drink from Sagan's hand without protest and placed the tumbler on a side table. He tasted like Christmas trees when I stuck my tongue in his mouth. His arms tightened around my waist, his kiss lustful, his cock growing against my ass. That was good. He wanted me and I wanted his cock inside me again, even if he said no to our play tonight. The fabric of my dress bunched in his fist. "Is that a yes?" I said in his mouth.

He pulled away. "Yes, I want you, us, together."

"You understand Carter will lead?" I said, "Are you still alright with three?"

He looked past me at Carter. "I'm ready, let's do this."

In two strides Carter stood in front of us. His fingers curled around my arm, yanking me to my feet. Sagan, alarmed, shot up from the chair, an objection on his face. I shook my head, mouthing 'no' to Sagan. I knew better than to protest this treatment. I had the bastard Carter tonight.

Carter ignored his concern. I was his, and he would decide how much of me he would share. He slid his hands down my arms, taking my palms, and he kissed them, slipping them around his neck, bringing me close to kiss me. I melted into his lips, the taste of champagne heady. He lifted a panel of the dress away, exposing me. I wasn't wearing panties or bra. He didn't provide them. Carter knew exactly how he wanted me to look. He wanted easy access to whatever he wanted. He roughly pushed two fingers into my pussy. I winced, then breathed in when he went deep. "You're so wet and ready for this," he whispered into my ear.

Sagan discarded his jacket and tie. He released a few buttons and eased back into the chair, his eyes bright, anticipating what was to come. We locked stares when I was turned to face him. Carter was behind me, nuzzling my neck. I leaned into him, enjoying his hands playing with me through the fabric until he settled at the deep V of my dress. I sensed tension in his fingers as they gripped the edge of the neckline. In a sudden violent action, he ripped the one seam open, and the tearing threads popped with the force until I was free and stood naked in diamonds, sapphires, and blue stilettos, the dredges of my dress pooled at my feet.

His fingers searched my hair for the clip. He pulled, releasing my hair to cascade to my shoulders. His hand skimmed my hip. The familiar touch was sensual, as his other large hand found my breast, cupping it, weighing the heaviness. "Stand straighter," he spoke into my ear. "Let him see everything." I pulled my shoulders back, my chest lifted. "I will miss my beautiful Shelby," he said to Sagan. "I was her first and had the pleasure of training her. She was a willing, talented student. God, the things my princess will do to please."

Sagan watched us, entranced, his bulge visible, his hands aching to take himself out. Carter's hand brushed my cheek. "Help him out, princess, but don't make him come, not yet. Remember, I lead. And Sagan, she doesn't come until I say." Carter released me and nudged me forward. "On your knees."

My nervous fingers unbuckled the belt, button, and zipper until I curled my fingers around Sagan's smooth, erect cock. I didn't wait for Carter's direction; I was too eager to taste him. I took him into my mouth as Carter moved close to my side. His hand stroked my hair, telling me I was sexy, encouraging me to please Sagan. "Relax," he soothed, while he fondled me between my legs, the sensation threatening my concentration. "That's right... Enjoy him."

Sagan groaned, urging me to take more of him. I accepted more and reached out for Carter. His cock already out, he guided my hand to him. I stroked him until Sagan began thrusting my mouth, my hold slipping from Carter. There was a tug on my arm. "Come to me," Carter said, "but continue to hold him." I pulled my mouth away but licked the head of Sagan's cock, lingering. "Do as I say," Carter urged, tightening his grip, pulling me away. "You'll have more of him later. Come here."

Carter in front of me, I transferred my mouth to his cock, taking him in. Sagan slipped from my grasp to take his place on his knees behind me. It was his turn to encourage me, touch me, while I gave my attention to Carter. He allowed me to please him, watching us at his feet until I thought he might break his rule and come, but he maintained his control while I worked. He finally caressed my face, then withdrew. I looked for his approval that I had done well, but instead he scooped me up and headed for the bedroom, placing me on the bed. I pulled at Carter's shirt, helping him to undress. I kept an eye on Sagan as he pulled off his clothes, trying to keep my excitement down.

Carter stood, pulling me from the bed, my back to him. He gently unclasped the necklace, while Sagan carefully removed my earrings and bracelet. I slipped out of my heels, the absence of four inches noticeable. We were close, the heat of their bodies sensual, their hands stroking, touching me.

Carter returned to the bed, back to the pillows at the headboard. "Shelby, come to me," he said, his hand outstretched. Tucking myself between his legs, I placed the flat of my hands on either side of his hips, moving down to finish sucking him. He tilted my face up and kissed me. "Turn around and rest on my chest." He motioned Sagan to the bed.

Sagan knelt on the bed, looking down at me, hair in his face. He pushed my legs apart to lie between them. His light kiss grazed my mouth. I responded, and he gave me more of his lips until he moved away to leave kisses on my neck, between my breasts, grazing my belly, stopping at my thighs. Sagan's lips at my sex, I writhed, already imagining his kiss. "Shelby," Carter said as his big hands massaged my breasts. "Let him take his time."

Sagan's fingers opened my slit, and his soft, wet tongue made slow passes until it settled on my clit. They were tentative kisses at first that changed to his probing tongue, building my orgasm with each touch until I clutched the bed, struggling not to give in to my body. Carter held me tight. "Enjoy it, don't come," he warned.

"I can't…" I gasped. I was in reach of letting go.

Carter pulled me back, breaking my contact. Sagan lifted his head. I reached for my clit; Carter pushed my hand away. "I said, not yet." Sagan jostled to his knees.

"I need it, Carter," I said, "I need to release!"

Carter shoved me to the side of the bed. I rolled onto my front, dazed by his reaction. Carter walked to the side of the bed and pulled me to the edge. His hand came down hard on my ass. The sound shot through the room.

Sagan got to his feet. "Shit, Carter," he said, confronting him. "It's only fun. Let her come."

Carter drew his attention to Sagan. The men were of equal height and power. Father and son with the same will. It would be explosive if allowed to ignite. "You agreed I would lead," came Carter's reply. Sagan stepped closer.

I moved between them, facing Sagan. "It's part of it," I whispered to him. "He won't hurt me, he never has." Although that spank was a little harder than usual. Red blooming across my behind, I pulled Sagan's hand to my ass. "Spank me." He looked at me. "Take me over your knee," I said, pleading with him, afraid he might stop. This was nothing compared to our regular play. He placed his arm around my waist and kissed me, gaze still on Carter.

"Is it settled?" Carter brushed a possessive hand over my arm. Sagan nodded.

Carter pulled me away, his hand stroking my cheek, searching my face. "Are you alright, princess, do you want to go on?"

"Yes," I touched his hand. "Don't worry, I'm fine. You know I would tell you."

He checked me again, still deciding. He kissed my hair. "Good, get back on the bed and ride him."

Pushing Sagan on the bed, I mounted him. Carter stood by the bed, watching. Sagan's gaze followed me as I moved my hips. His concerns gone, he slid his hands up and down my thighs. Carter opened the side table, taking out a tube. The lube was cold when he applied it to my hole, sliding his finger in, preparing me to receive him. Sagan was in a haze, my pussy filled with him, enjoying him under me while Carter watched. I smiled and reached out for him to join us.

Carter moved onto the bed. My heart raced. Two men so close, their musky scent thick around me. I could orgasm just on the scent of men and sex. I wanted this so badly. I wanted them to use every part of me.

Carter was pushing at my hole. I panicked, but his arms went around me. "Relax, let me inside."

I leaned back to his chest, his hand squeezing my breast. I stopped moving my hips. Sagan watched, brushing my thighs, waiting for Carter to enter me from behind, waiting for us to be three. "Let me in, Shelby." His lips were close to my ear. Carter dropped his fingers to my clit and I moaned softly. I willed my body to relax, although this moment was delicious too, the moment before I surrendered. But his cock was insistent, only his head entered at first, gaining a little more each time he probed until he was inside.

They were both in me, using me for their pleasure, for my pleasure. This was a dream. They grunted, swore, and struggled as they pumped me in a wild fever. I kept my mind in this moment, not daring to go beyond this bed. I was wild too in their wanting me, holding on to this happiness for as long as I could. I prolonged the pleasure until I couldn't hold it any longer. I came in a blur of sensation, screaming my release with Sagan and Carter climaxing just after me.

They remained inside me, my body a tight bond between us until they moved away, leaving me lost. Carter gathered me to him, holding me close to his chest while Sagan kissed me, telling me I was beautiful. I smiled at them. They were beautiful and if I had enough courage, I would tell them that I loved them. I wanted us to stay like this, suspended always together. Sagan took his turn holding me, his arms around me, whispering. They let me know I was wanted, loved, desired.

I was between them now, heated by their big bodies. Hands were touching me, mouths kissing and tasting. I was electric in my wanting more of them. I would not sleep tonight.

CHAPTER 11

Reprieve

$\mathcal{I}$ woke in the early morning with Sagan next to me face down, clutching the pillow and breathing softly. *God, he's sexy, stretched out like a cat, his black hair in his face, big biceps flexing as he sleeps.* If I turned him over, I was sure he'd have a hard on. I wanted to touch him, to wake him with my hand on his cock, but I wouldn't disturb his perfection. I settled in to watch him for a while.

I finally turned away from him to rest on my back, stretching away the soreness from last night. I was thinking about a long, hot, lavender-scented soak in a very hot tub at my house. Carter stirred; he was on his back, eyes open. He put his arm around me and pulled me to him and gave me a kiss. "Good morning, princess."

Raising onto an elbow, he looked over at Sagan. Dropping his hand to the floor, he picked up a shirt, throwing it at Sagan's head. "Get up, you need to go home. I'll talk to you later."

Sagan pulled the shirt off his head and lifted himself from the pillow, still blurry-eyed, looking at me, flashing his devil's grin.

"Good morning, sunshine." He leaned over, kissed me, and pulled my hair. "I'll call you later." He walked around the room, picking up clothing on his way out. "I'll use the other bathroom," he called over his shoulder.

CHAPTER 12

Goodbye Girl

*C*arter is not the CEO of Folio; the press has no interest in his life. We are safe dining in public. We've finished our long, awkward breakfast and I'm of two minds. I want to stay as long as I can with him to hold these moments, but something tells me I need to leave to start a difficult beginning. There are no more arguments to make, no more time left; we are at the end. I know he still loves me and that last night was for me. I nearly break down when I think of what he did for my happiness. How can this be over, when all I see is love in his eyes? How could he think anyone could replace him?

We leave the restaurant holding hands, both having difficulty stopping the stray tears that plague us. Carter is in profile, brows furrowed as he gazes down the street. I smile at this complex man; for all his directness, his brashness, not many know he is sentimental and tender.

The brightness of the day warms my face as we stroll and I wish for a gray depressing drizzle of rain, so no one can see me hurting.

We came to this place separately, so we say goodbye here on a nearly deserted side street. He holds me tight, I cling to him, breathing him in, still hoping I could change this, but it feels final, like it is the last time. We kiss with all the passion of our ten years together. Reluctant when we break apart, he is still close enough to touch.

He looks down at me. The man who's been my whole world dazzles me with his sad, brilliant smile. "I love you, Shelby Oberman, and I always will." Before I can respond, he turns and strides down the road, my heart tearing with each step, but I will myself to watch him leave.

He is too far away to hear me when I remember to say, "I love you, Carter Morrison, and I always will."

The End

EPILOGUE

Sagan

’ve never been to Montreal. The city is alive with energy, art, and music. I wish I could stay longer to explore the city, but I need to be in New York tomorrow. I sit in an open-air café, waiting, watching people. Then I see him in the crowd. He's walking toward me, his stride not as urgent. After a year, his face is a little thinner. His eighty-watt smile is still the same. I stand. "Good to see you, Carter." I hold out my hand, he takes it and pulls me into a hug, thumping my back twice with his big hand.

"How's Shelby?"

He waits for my answer as we take our seats and order our coffees. "She's good," I say, but I know he wants more. "How are you?" I ask.

He looks out at the busy street. "Better now that I'm done with this phase. I hear she's doing well at Folio, but not much more."

I'm reluctant to talk about Shelby. I don't want to contribute to his pain, but his stare says he needs to know. "She had a rough time of it after you left," I say. "She'd come over to stay in my guest room. Sometimes I'd hear her crying at night." He looks away, but I still catch the hurt in his eyes. Maybe I shouldn't have said that; he has enough to worry about.

"Are you together now?" He says this with apprehension. I don't know if he really wants to know this.

Our coffees arrive.

"You're a hard act to follow, Carter." He smiles at that. "No, I wouldn't say we're together. Right now, we're just fuck buddies. She comes over and lets me take care of her when she doesn't want to be alone. I've asked her to move in with me, to have a real relationship, but she says she's not ready."

"Be patient with her; you have all the time in the world." I can see he's not over her. I've seen the same look in Shelby's eyes. "I know about you and Cecile," Carter says. He tosses this out like it's another mundane topic and not something that changed his life.

"I wondered when you were going to find out."

"Once I figured out you were the man in the photo, it wasn't hard to press Cecile for the truth. I've got to say you have my DNA for manipulation."

I researched Carter before I came to Silicon Valley. I'd done it before, but this was a more aggressive pass into his background. I was curious about his wife; there was little about her and she rarely appeared with Carter in public. I tracked her down and met her at a charity auction. We became friends, someone I could talk to about Carter, but I told her early on I was his son.

"She asked me to help," I said. "It didn't go the way we planned, but it did make it easier for you to make a choice."

He considers me. "For someone I didn't raise, you're a lot like me." He leans back, throwing his gaze across the street. "Life is never predictable," he begins. "Before Cecile outed me about my affair, I'd already planned to leave my wife. I wanted to see Shelby with my ring on her finger holding our daughter. At least in all my imaginings it was a little girl we had together. I think I wanted to make up for being a crap father." He gives me a weak smile, then sighs. "But you're right, my cancer put things into perspective. I'd planned to propose to Shelby the night I returned from Washington. We were about to talk when you called. Funny, the doctor gave me the news during your conversation with Shelby. Just like that," he snaps his fingers, "my plans were shot to hell." He took a breath. "I knew I'd be in for a hard fight and I couldn't ask her to be with me. I needed time to think after I got the news. I left her a note promising to talk later instead of facing her. Then Cecile files for divorce..." He trails off, looking into his coffee. "I love Shelby, but I had to give her a chance at a life I know she wants, one I can't give her."

"Is that why you've adopted a buzz cut?" I say.

He laughs and pulls a hand over what is barely more than peach fuzz. "I looked like a billiard ball a few months ago. It's growing back grayer, but it's all there."

"Cecile was giving you a way out of your marriage," I said. "That's why she tried to divorce you and name Shelby in the action. But you chose to stay with your wife. The photo was easy enough to arrange. Our builds are the same. I had a photographer buddy snap the picture. He caught Shelby and I leaving a restaurant together on the way to an industry association meeting."

He's silent, taking this in, then looks over at me, something still not quite set in his mind. "But you're in love with Shelby; why did you agree to help Cecile?"

It was my turn to look away, not wanting him to see the flash of emotion threatening to overtake me. "Because I had five years to get her away from you," I said.

There's no place like home after a long trip. I drag myself into the house and see the pile of mail on the kitchen counter. Shelby's been here housesitting while I was gone. I called Mrs. Grandville, who is dog sitting Eugene, and asked her to keep him one more night. She's the owner of Verdot, the standard French Poodle two doors down and Eugene's best friend.

I open a bottle of wine and sit on the couch. I'm so tired I can only muster enough energy to turn on music. Forget the news, I'm not up to watching that shit show tonight. I fall asleep and I dream of Shelby. I see her a lot in my dreams. I see flashes of her walking, smiling, but I can never find her.

"Mr. Miller." Someone is shaking me.

"Sagan, get up!"

Something is burning. I open my eyes. Shelby is standing over me, distressed. "You need to come now!" she yells.

Groggy, I stumble after her into the kitchen. A pan is on fire. I can't get close enough to smother it. She's trying to explain, grabbing the flour to throw on the flames. I knock the canister out of her hand and drag her away. The fire alarm is going crazy, and smoke belches out of the kitchen. I run to the garage for the fire extinguisher and pray that it isn't too old to work. I pull the pin and let out a spray that douses the fire.

"What the fuck, Shelby, what happened?" I say, still not fully awake. Then I realize she's shaken. I put my arm around her. "Don't worry, I needed to remodel the kitchen anyway."

She laughs. "You were dead to the world when I came in; you didn't even hear me call your name. I know you hadn't eaten, so I thought I would make you scrambled eggs."

I glance back at the kitchen. "Looks like it got away from you. Why didn't you tell me you were coming?"

"I wanted to surprise you."

"You did that." She was probably lonely while I was away and wanted to cuddle.

"No, you don't understand." She takes my hand and pulls me along to my bedroom.

"Open the closet." I push the door open and her clothes are in there.

"I wanted to tell you that I'm ready."

I kiss her; I'm fully awake. She pulls away and leaves the room. When she returns, she has the bottle of wine and two glasses. We toast. "To Sagan and Shelby," she says, and we touch glasses and take a sip. Shelby takes my glass away and places it on the end table.

"There's something else I have to tell you."

I don't think I can take any more excitement. "What is it?"

"I've given away all those women's clothes in your guest room."

"I think my relatives will understand," I say, giving her a grin. She gives me a yeah-right look.

We laugh.

Shelby steps forward, places her hands on my chest, and pushes me onto the bed. I grab her wrist on the way down and she falls on top of me.

"Okay, Mr. Miller," she says, "now fuck me sideways."

<<<<>>>>

LOVE CONTRACT

Read an excerpt from book two of the *Love at Work* series

CHAPTER 1

The Interview

I make a U-turn, just barely making it through the yellow arrow light, and nearly careen into a red Tesla. That A-hole of a driver had, like a fish, gotten in front of me when he made a right turn. He's probably thinking it's his right to cut me off because he has a trendier car than me. The flat of my hand hits the steering wheel with a frustrated thump. I hate these jumped-up Ford Focuses. Traffic at 9:15 a.m. in San Jose is a beast and I'm going to be late.

I crane my neck to see addresses on the buildings and try to keep an eye on the stop-and-go traffic in front of me. "Goddamn it, it's got to be around here somewhere," I say to no one. I check the clock on the dashboard. I'm quickly burning my twenty-minute cushion trying to find this freaking place. The GPS app on my phone, which is sitting in my cup holder, is directing my progress. The male Aussie voice that's giving me directions just landed me in front of an auto dealership.

I should have done a dry run and made sure I knew where this place was before today. Chalk it up to arrogance. I was born in this valley and know every freaking nook and cranny from Morgan Hill to San Francisco and beyond. I've forgotten that they're building up every spare inch of this place. If you didn't drive someplace for more than a month, there would be two new malls, lofts, and a trendy hamburger place you've never seen but you just realize you're dying to try.

"Okay, people," I say, trying to calm myself before I do something stupid. "I just need to find a building on North First Street and no one will be harmed in the process." I brake and make a hard right into a parking lot to text the recruiter who set up my interview. When I look over at the building I've parked in front of, I realize glory-be-hallelujah if it's not the place I'm looking for. I swing into a visitor's spot and kill the engine. I grab my bag and tablet and speed-walk across the parking lot.

Just before I get to the lobby, a guy walks out of the building and takes a few steps away from the door. As I get closer, I register that he's a tall hunk of gorgeousness. Mr. Sexy catches me going full throttle towards the entrance and doubles back to open the door as I sail into the lobby, a "Thanks" thrown over my shoulder as I pass him. He gives me a deep, rumbled "No problem" that has some mirth hidden underneath it. I ignore him.

I'm nearly out of breath when I reach the security station. A bored, rail-thin male, somewhere south of sixty with a black tie that seems to be wearing him, stares up at me while his fingers tap something on his keyboard. "Welcome to Drachen Technology."

I smile, only because I'm winded and need a second. "I'm here to see Melanie Madrone, I—"

"Name," he says, not stopping his typing.

"Kellis Ivarsson."

"Driver's license, please."

I fish in my purse, open my wallet, and hand him the license while taking in the lobby. It's an ultra-modern reception area of glass and steel that says "yeah, we're a bad ass technology company in Silicon Freaking Valley." The predominate colors are stark grays with splashes of cold blues. Behind the gleaming white enamel security station, the familiar dragon logo of Drachen Technology, a multi-national company headquartered in Germany, looms its dark dominance, seeing all.

The security man slides a badge and my license toward me. "You'll need this to enter the offices. The badge is only good for the day. Ms. Madrone will be down shortly."

I retrieve the badge and my ID. I lean forward to see Robert Benson on his name tag. "Thank you, Robert," I say and follow it up with a smile.

He doesn't look up from his screen. "You're welcome, Ms. Ivarsson."

That reply sounds formal. He's probably building security, not a Drachen employee.

I find a seat, when I spy the man who opened the door is still standing outside, watching me through the glass. He gives me a ghost of a grin, then nods. I don't manage a smile, but I return the nod. I thought he might come into the lobby to speak with me, but I guess this brief exchange is enough for him. He begins striding down the path to the parking lot. It occurs to me to ask Robert who he was, but I decide it isn't an option. After my epic break-up with Tim, I'm not about to run after a man, no matter how hot he looks. I've sworn off men, at least for a while.

The black leather sofa I settle on looks nicer than comfortable. I've made it here with five minutes to spare. I pull out my cell phone and run through my texts. There's one from my sister Chloe, who asks me to pick up pizza after I get off from work. I'm working, but as a volunteer at a local job club in an adult education complex. I teach a series of classes on how to find a job. However, the funny thing is that I don't have a job at the moment, but I hope to remedy that after my interview at Drachen.

Today, my topic for my class will be on how to interview. I make a quick note to cover knowing where the interview is located beforehand.

"Kellis?"

A woman in her thirties, about five inches over five feet, bobbed coffee-color hair, and large cornflower eyes, smiles at me. "Melanie?"

"Yes, welcome," she says, extending her hand.

I shake her delicate palm.

"Do you need anything before we start? Water or the restroom?"

"I'm good," I reply. I follow her into an elevator that takes us to the level below. She taps on the light to reveal abandoned cubes, with equipment still in them. It's clear no one has occupied these seats for a while. It looks like IT is using this floor for equipment storage. We walk through the center row of cubicles, heading for a glassed-in meeting room. To the left of the space is a large area with two screens, video equipment, and about fifteen rows of chairs. Melanie observes me looking at the area.

"We use this space for our all-hands meetings," she says, flicking on a light to illuminate the area. "This building is actually the headquarters for the company in the Americas. We have about twelve other sites around the country, including Puerto Rico. One screen is used to project the speaker's image to the room, while the other is for us to see the other sites that are participating in the meeting. If someone is speaking from, let's say, San Antonio, the speaker's image can be seen by everyone in the meeting. It's one way we keep in contact with other sites."

"Is this floor used for storage?" I say, looking at an old calendar that's still tacked to the outside of a cube.

"This housed a division that was sold almost two years ago. Many of the employees now work for the new company. Drachen hasn't decided if we will acquire another business or find a smaller space." She pushes open the door to the meeting room. A couple of monitors sit on the table. Melanie frowns and picks up a monitor, and I grab the other.

"Just place that one over here," she instructs. "Sorry, I cleaned this area; someone must have sneaked in here for a quick meeting." She sighs. "Please have a seat."

I settle in, and my nerves jump to attention. "Remember," I chide myself, "what you'd tell your candidates in prep: 'Don't think of this as an interview; think of it as a chat with your friend.'"

She folds her hands. "I'm the manager of staffing and a few other related functions. When the team reviewed your resume, we were impressed with your background, but why would someone who owned a staffing company want to work as a corporate recruiter?"

I'm surprised she asks this question early in the interview. If I was hiring a recruiter to be on my team, who is clearly overqualified, that would be my first question.

I make eye contact with my potential employer, who appears poised and in control. "The recession hit all of us hard," I begin. "I had large corporations for clients, but when they stopped hiring, I was forced to close shop."

That was the diplomatic way of saying it. But the hard truth was the gravy train came to a screeching halt when I discovered companies were posting jobs with no intention of hiring. They used the time to cut the fat, pare down benefits, and let go of the workers they really wanted to see the back of. They held on to their precious remaining employees and hunkered down to ride out the storm.

"I did a few years as a business consultant," I say, continuing my rehearsed response, "but when the market came back to life, I wanted to return and do what I do best: placing great candidates in jobs and companies they love." I stop talking. Number one rule of interviewing is to answer the question, then shut up and wait for the next one. I've had a few candidates that I've prepped ignore my rule and talk their way out of a job because they couldn't stand silence.

She doesn't appear convinced. "Why not re-open the business?"

"That's a fair question. I've been out of staffing for a few years. Restarting would be like opening a new business. The players are different, new industries are hot, I would have to pipeline candidates, which takes time, and even build a new client base. That would take a lot more time. Truthfully, I've done that and was successful, but now I'm looking for a new challenge. Mostly so I wouldn't have to deal with managing recruiters, payroll, worker's compensation, or dozens of other things as a single owner."

"If you were hired here, you'd have to do the same things."

"It's different. I would only have one client and I'd be pipelining as Drachen's recruiter. Candidates will talk to a corporate recruiter faster because they are a direct line to the company. An agency recruiter may or may not have a contract with the company they are working with."

The left side of her mouth quirks up. I score a point. Rule number fifteen: forget about your nerves and observe your interviewer. Unless they're a poker player, you can always gauge where you stand. We chat for an hour, which was more like a strategy meeting. After my last answer, Melanie produces her phone and checks it. "Sorry, my time went over a little and I'm late for a meeting," she says, making a few taps on her cell.

I start to gather my stuff, grateful I'll have some time before my class to relax.

"I'll send the next interviewer down," she says, glancing up from her phone. "I've let Haley, our coordinator, know; she's managing the interviewers. She may come down to check on you. Let her know if you need anything."

I stop collecting my things. *Wait a minute, what?*

She must have responded to the surprise on my face. "Didn't Candice tell you? You have four interviews."

No, and I'm going to kill that absent-minded recruiter. She assured me I'd be speaking with the manager when she arranged this interview. It was supposed to be a quick hour in and out with Melanie Madrone, who I researched to an inch of her life. Candice broke rule number five: know who you're going to speak to before the interview so you can do your research on that person. Interviewers could be anyone from members of a team to a wild card like a VP; either way, I was going to have to wing it.

I drop my bag and plaster a smile on my face. "Yes, she did," I lie. "I was going to ask where the restrooms are on this floor." Three hours later, I'm escorted back to the lobby. I'm surprised it's still daylight.

CHAPTER 2

Pizza Pizza

he pizza box is threatening to tip out of my outstretched hand as my purse slides from my elbow to the wrist, and the fingers of my other hand are trying to push the key into the lock. I manage to open the door to the house without incident. The TV is on, every square inch of floor is taken up with stacks of paper, and there's no one in sight.

"Chloe," I yell, pushing the door closed with my hip, "I've got pizza, come out."

"I'm on the phone," comes the reply from her room.

I place the pizza box and my purse on the kitchen table. Chloe arrives in an oversize T-shirt, jeans, and no shoes. Her dark hair is pulled back into a ponytail. Even with no make-up, I've seen guys give her a second look. She has big brown eyes and a full mouth like our mother. She is much shorter than me and carries her weight in her hips. That full mouth is now frowning at me.

"What?" I say, trying to figure out why my big sister is disapproving.

She points to my bag. "Your purse doesn't belong there."

"It's only going to be there for a second."

"That's what you said about that box in the corner two weeks ago and it's still there."

I pick up the bag and head for my room with my sister on my heels.

"How did the interview go?" she asks.

I pitch the bag on the desk and kick off my heels. My sister sits on the foot of the bed cross-legged. I pull off my shirt and skirt. I take a T-shirt from a pile of clean clothes I've yet to fold and push my head through the opening. "Did you wash this in hot water?" I say, trying to get it over my chest.

My sister looks at me critically. "No. Do you think they've grown? Maybe you could transplant some of what you've got on top down to your butt. It might balance you out so you don't look like you're about to tip over," she says and smiles sweetly.

I give her the evil eye and pull on my sweat bottoms. I look like my dad, Zach Ivarsson, who is over six feet. He's a professional bowler who always places in the top five on the money board. My first childhood memory is of my father encouraging me while I pushed a bowling ball down an alley.

I have long, dark hair like Chloe, but I usually wear it in a braid down my back. I'm tall, but not as tall as my dad, with long legs and long limbs, busty with small hips. I loom over Chloe, who is displaying a grin like she is ready to burst. I place my hands on my hips; I'm not letting her get away with the old taunt.

"Dear sister," I say, "you're just mad because you were blessed with mosquito bites and have boob envy."

Chloe's eyes widen, then she rocks back on the bed holding her side, laughing. "Good one, Kel," she says barely getting the words out. "I still say you should be a comedian or at least write comedy."

"I'm glad I keep you amused. Let's eat, I'm starving." I walk out of the room, her laughter trailing me.

I hand my sister a beer and she gives me a napkin. I drop into a chair. The open pizza box is wafting heavenly aromas. I shove a big piece of Johnny's Pi Explosion in my mouth and I'm finally a happy camper.

"Kel?"

"Hmmm?" I say. I swallow and I'm about to take another bite.

Chloe looks down at her chest and considers. "Do you think I have mosquito bites?"

"No, you're just right."

She grins. "I spoke to Gwen next door," she says, then tilts her beer up for a drink.

I stop chewing and swallow. Chloe always knows what's going on in the court. The neighbors volunteer all kinds of information to her because my sister has an honest face and she cares about people. "What's the earth-shattering news… did someone get an electric lawn mower?"

She ignores me. "Gwen, Tom and the kids are moving by the end of the week. He's got a job in Colorado. They're renting the house until they decide whether to sell."

That means new neighbors. I was going to miss Gwen and Tom, but not their three yappy dogs. I point my pizza slice toward the living room. "Why are there stacks of papers in there?"

She looks over as if she'd forgotten the place looks like a "how to be a hoarder" training video. "I've got to put together a report for the counsel." She sighs.

Chloe works as an analyst for small city government. Her boss is some councilman who doesn't know how to turn on the copier. She's always stuck with administrative tasks, although they have two perfectly good admins that have been there since the Clinton administration. San Pacitas is an excellent-run city, but they seem to be in the mid-fifties when it comes to the actual governing. I'm just glad we don't live there.

"How many trees did you kill as a result of this report?" I ask, taking another bite. This pizza is really good.

"Several, but to their credit, it's recycled paper. I'm not going to bore you with the city's intrigue. It really is too stupid to repeat. Tell me about your interview."

I recall the story between sips of beer and bites of pizza. "They seem to be nice people," I admit, "although I was consigned to an underground lair during my interview."

She takes a drag on her beer, then stifles a burp. "Sorry." She looks surprised by the noise. "If they offered you the job, would you want to work there?"

I shrug and close the pizza box. "I've never worked for a company that big before. I ran my business alone for a very long time; it might be nice not having to make every decision. Yeah, I think it might be interesting."

"Did you see any cute engineers?" That's Chloe, always trying to help my pathetic love life.

"I only talked to females. Wait a minute, I take that back. I did talk to a security guard." I'm not going to tell her about the hottie outside of Drachen's reception that stared holes into me or she'll never stop asking questions about him.

"Then if you think you'd like it there, I was talking to Candice, your recruiter, when you came in. She says they want to offer you the job."

I sit back in my chair. "Why didn't you tell me this earlier?"

"I know you." She sniffs. "If you hated the place, you would have taken the job anyway. I wanted to know how you felt about them before I told you in case I had to talk you out of taking the offer."

"I would not," I complain, then stop. "Okay, you're right. But in my defense, I need the money; I'm dipping too far into my savings. I was going to have to take something soon."

She waves a hand toward me. "Your soul would have died."

That is enough of my big sister telling me how to run my life. Just because she was right about ex Tim doesn't mean she's allowed to make my decisions. "Careful, you're sounding like Mom."

She lets the comment sail right over her, and instead she doubles down. "You're not the corporate type; bureaucracy is going to make you insane. I say open another business or, better yet, work for Mom. She'd love that."

"You're crazy," I say, defending my position. She's right; I might not be the corporate type, but I want to try. I have to prove to myself I could do this. "If you can do it, I certainly can, what's the big deal?"

She takes a few seconds to respond. "I'm made of stronger stuff; besides, I don't take them seriously or I would have opened a vein long ago."

CHAPTER 3

First Day

$\mathcal{I}$ follow Melanie down a row of cubes, getting the who's-this-person stare from the cube community. At least I'm able to make it to a floor where it is populated with people. We halt at her office, something small with one wall glassed that affords her the back view of a bank of cubicles. She can see her team... well, if they step out of their boxes.

"I'm glad you're here. The rest of the team is anxious to meet you," she says.

What rest of the team? I thought they'd sent everyone downstairs to grill me during the interview.

She opens a drawer. "I have some information I want to share with you." Pulling out an Excel sheet, she places it on her desk.

"Sorry to interrupt," says a woman with a blond pixie cut who enters the office. "You asked me to tell you when they're ready. Everyone is in the conference room."

Melanie's gaze snaps to the door. "Kellis, this is your coordinator, Haley. She sits in front of you. Haley will show you how things work here. We will eventually need another recruiter and I hope working with you will help with her training. We plan to find her replacement once she's ready to take the new role."

"Great to meet you," Haley says with a wide smile.

"You as well," I return, grateful I have someone to help me with staffing.

Melanie pushes away from the desk. "We can finish our meeting later. Let's leave now; you're invited as well. This little get-together will give you a chance to see us informally."

We enter a conference room filled with balloons and crepe paper stuck around a sign that says, "Double the pleasure, double the fun, double the joy with a girl and a boy." About fifteen people are seated around a conference table chatting. In the middle of the huge table is a cake frosted pink and blue.

"Abigail's having twins," Haley says. "Ah, there are no seats; let's stand here near the door, and we can grab chairs from another room once the party begins."

A few seconds later, two people are engaged in a heated discussion outside the closed door. A male is trying to convince someone that they need her report now. It sounds like he's losing the argument.

"Oh my God," Haley says in an exasperated whisper, "she's leaving... open the door."

Others are silently urging me. "Go ahead," someone whispers. "Open it now!"

I grab the handle and give it a quick jerk. A very pregnant Abigail and the man are staring at me. I don't know what to say; I step back to reveal the people in the room, who jump up and scream "surprise."

Abigail's mouth drops open. She covers it with her hand and shrieks. Laughter erupts, and she makes thank yous to the room while she takes in the decorations. I think she's going to cry until Haley moves forward and places an arm around her.

I stay by the door. I only know Melanie and Haley. After the excitement calms down, I'll attempt to introduce myself to some of the approachable ones, if Melanie or Haley forget about me.

"You must be the new recruiter," comes a male voice from behind me.

The man who'd arrived with Abigail is moving toward me. I hadn't paid attention to him before, but now I have time to really notice him. He's the guy who opened the door for me the day I interviewed at Drachen. This time, he gives me a real smile, and extends his hand. "I'm Matt."

I look up into blue-gray eyes, at dark hair swept back from his forehead, light stubble on a strong jaw, and I almost forget to shake his hand. I wonder if he recognizes me from the day I was here for my interview. I stretch out my hand to shake his palm and an electric shock shoots through my fingers. We both recoil.

"Sorry," he says, looking at his flexing hand, "that's never happened before."

I recover first. "No worries. I'm Kellis, by the way."

He steps closer. "Then you are the new recruiter. Great, we're going to be working together. I supervise the production line in South San Jose facility. We're adding a temporary night shift and I'm going to need help staffing that crew."

God, he smells good. I know he's speaking, but all I can do is look up, breathe him in, and nod. He's in a pair of dark jeans and dress shirt. That isn't unusual around here; I'd met the CEO and he was wearing something similar. There's no ring on Matt's finger, but that doesn't mean anything.

"I'm in the office today for a meeting," he says, breaking into my thoughts. "But when you settle in, I'd like to set up a meeting with you to see the facility and tour the production line."

It might be nice working with a hot production supervisor. Then I remember another rule that doesn't even have a number. It's my dad's when I first started working and he'd notice I was getting a bit too excited about a co-worker. "Kellis, don't get your honey where you get your money," was his stern warning. It's a stupid rhyme, but it sticks in my head when it looks like I might be wandering into dangerous territory with someone who should be off limits. He warned me dating someone at work never turns out well. Someone always has to leave after the break-up and that's usually the woman. Matt stops talking. He gives me a curious look. I smile and nod. Idiot me lost the thread of the conversation.

"Okay, well, I'll catch up with you later," he says. "It's nice meeting you." Matt faces the crowded conference room. "I'm late for a meeting," he announces.

"Ah, can't you stay for cake? It's chocolate, your favorite," a woman says with a pleading smile.

"You got me," he says with a grin. "It's my favorite and, believe me, if I stay, I'll eat half that cake, but I can't." He turns his attention to the very pregnant woman. "And, Abigail, sorry about the rouse."

She beams. "Good one, Matt, I owe you for this."

"Well, if you want to pay me back, Abby," he spreads his hands wide, "Matthew is a nice name for a boy."

The conference room gives a collective groan. He throws a wave and strides out of the door.

Melanie moves me around the room, making introductions to the HR department. It will take a couple more interactions with them before I remember everyone's name. Melanie finally excuses us, and we stroll back to her office. This time, she instructs me to close the door to intruders.

"I see you've met Matt," she says, taking her seat.

"Yes, he asked me to help him staff a night crew," I say, swiping my notepad from the chair and sitting down.

"That's some of the information I want to share with you. It's a priority project, along with another."

"Is he the night supervisor for the production facility?"

Melanie wrinkles her nose. "Supervisor? He's the CEO of Dark Star. They are a subsidiary of Drachen Technology. He sold the company a few years ago but maintains the management of the company."

That's about the time I left the business. So that's Matt Westmore, one of the Valley's whiz kids who started a company out of college, found angel investors, and soon began to eat the lunches of all his competitors. That would have been another company I'd have gone after as a client, if I was still in business. They paid their vendors well and, in the company's early days, their partying and beer busts were legendary. They were one of the last companies of that era.

"The project I'm concerned about is for a VP from the home office, Kurt Heinrich," she says searching the paper work on her desk. "He's a rising star who's been assigned here to expand this region. He'll be heading a new division. He might bring some personnel with him, an admin and a manager, but he needs to fill out his team. You'll be working on the hiring of about six new team members." She pushes the sheet toward me. "This is a list of the jobs; the business partner assigned to his team has already worked with him to write the job descriptions."

I pick up the sheet and scan the information. "Is he available if I have questions?"

"That can be arranged. He isn't due in the US for another three weeks, but he'd like to start interviews next week on some of the sales positions."

I glance up from the sheet. "Does that mean we FaceTime?"

"Something like that. We have video equipment set up in a few of the conference rooms. You can have meetings and interviews there." She sits back in her chair. "I will warn you that it gets a bit tricky. Munich is about nine hours ahead of us. The sweet spot for you to meet with him will be 6-8 a.m. For him, it will be 3-5 p.m.

I grimace.

"He's made an exception for you; he's notorious for holding early-morning meetings. Unless you'd like to meet at 11 p.m. for his 6 a.m. meetings." She sighs. "Ah, the joys of midnight meetings. Just be glad we're not working on joint hiring with the Bangalore team."

I'm not a morning person; it was a problem when I managed my company. A lot of recruiting is done after work; at least, it is for me. Candidates seem more receptive after an unhappy day at work.

Melanie gives me a half-hearted smile. "You're meeting with him tomorrow at 6 a.m. Haley will go over how to use the video equipment. Good news is that you'll become a pro at it."

CHAPTER 4

Munich Calling

Most of the meeting rooms in the dungeon, that's my new name for the lower level where I was interviewed, are equipped with video equipment. There are only a handful of early birds working this morning on the main floors, but no one is here on the lower level.

Blurry-eyed and sipping from a mug of coffee, I try to wake up enough to be alert for my meeting with Kurt Heinrich. Thank God Haley walked me through the set-up yesterday; it seems straightforward, so I should have no problems. I tuck my folder of notes for the meeting under my arm and move inside the small conference room. I turn on the light and discover someone has used this room for a meeting after we cleaned. No one is outside the room; there's no one around to hear my complaints. Later, I'll post a sign, warning under pain of death, not to use this room to scare any would-be meeting room wreckers. There's no reason for this carnage; there are enough spaces to choose from around here.

I check my phone. I have ten minutes to move monitors and cups off the table and re-set up the video console. At least the camera and the screen aren't disturbed. The camera casts a wide angle to include most of the room. If teams are meeting, everyone in the room can be visible to the camera. I deposit the cups in the trash and notice a large coffee spill on the table. I don't have time to find a paper towel to wipe it clean. I place my mug near the puddle to remind me to avoid it and test the console. I dial the number to the bridge to call up Kurt's conference room, but no picture appears. I pull the cheat sheet from my training session with Haley. I'd followed her instructions and all the lights are flashing except for the one next to the picture icon. Maybe it's the connection. I push the chair aside, drop to all fours, and crawl underneath the table, trying to sort out, from the tangle of wires, which is the right one. There's no one to ask and I'm feeling like an idiot until I see the plug and shove it into the power strip.

"Guten Morgen, Ms. Ivarsson," comes a disembodied voice. "I assume that's you, but I can only see your backside. Did you lose something?"

Shit, there's a big thump when my head hits the table's underside. Great, I'm going to have a goose egg on my head. I crawl out to see the image of an impeccably dressed man peering down at me. The feed is clear. I'm sure he can see me just as well. He's seated in a conference room. The diffused after-4 p.m. lighting makes him look like a black and white photograph. His dark, trendy European suit with the tie artfully loosened is just enough to signal this is the end of his day.

"Good afternoon. The equipment wasn't working," I say, slipping into my chair. I give him a tight smile to show I'm not fazed by our awkward introduction, but his blond GQ features are not pleased.

"Are you alright? It sounded like you hit your head. Are you well enough to continue?" His English is impeccable, like the rest of him.

He must have learned it from an English, not American, native speaker; there is only a slight German accent.

I want to rub my head, but I stifle the urge. I think a slight headache is beginning. I hope it isn't the result of a concussion. "I'm fine. How has your day been?" I ask.

"Good, Ms. Ivarsson. Did you receive my notes on the types of candidates I'm expecting?"

And the small talk and bonding period is now officially over; it's time to get down to business.

"Yes," I say, eyeing my folder a distance away. I lean out of my chair, resting my forearm on the table to retrieve the paperwork and pen. I slip back into my seat with the folder, but as I pull my arm away, a brown sticky stain blights most of the sleeve of my white shirt. I drop the file on my lap and keep my arm down.

"You seem to be having a bad day already. I hope that coffee wasn't hot." There didn't appear to be a lot of sympathy in his bored tone, just a statement of fact. "I can call someone to help you if you are injured," he offers. "If no one is there at this time of day," he glances at his watch, "I'm sure emergency services would respond."

Now he's just being an ass. "Thank you, Kurt, but I'm fine."

He appears to be ruffled. My tone was not unprofessional, and didn't I say thank you?

"As you wish. Are there any questions?"

"No, not at the moment," I say. "How can I contact you if I need to discuss candidates, interviews..."

"Anna Warner is my administrative assistant. Her details were in my notes to you. She will handle communications between us. Are there any more concerns?"

"No."

"Auf Wiedersehen, Fraulein Ivarsson." He nods and cuts the feed.

I stare at the blank screen. "Okay," I mumble, "I think that went well."

———— ✉ ————

The dark brown stain on my sleeve is now beige after my visit to the restroom. My team hadn't arrived yet. Haley would be in at eight and Melanie at nine. IT is still working on my computer. Since I don't have access to the company intranet, I decide to read through company marketing materials and notes from meetings on internal procedures. A little after eight, Melanie appears at my cube. She places her laptop case on the floor and adjusts her bag on her shoulder.

"I came in early to treat you to breakfast and discuss your meeting with Kurt. I've also got some new information on the night crew staffing for Dark Star. There's a place across the street. We can go there. How did it go? All sweetness and light I hope?"

"Is it legal to fire someone via video conference?" I say.

Melanie scrunches up her face. "Ouch, was it that bad? Never mind." She waves her hand to stop me. "Let's go now before the seats are all taken."

The little breakfast spot is filling up with diners. Melanie throws out some cheery hellos to some of the people that are standing in line waiting to order. It's a warm, bright morning and we're lucky to find a table outside. I relive my meeting with Kurt for Melanie's benefit between bites of muffin. I admit I told the story with a little more embellishment. I was channeling my mom's flare for drama. She valiantly tries to stifle a laugh at some of my tale, but a stray giggle manages to escape a couple of times.

"Have you ever met Kurt?" I ask.

"No, I almost slipped into your meeting this morning to meet him. I'd heard he looks like a blond footballer or what they call a soccer player here. He doesn't look the corporate type. Someone said he should be on the cover of something with those smoldering looks. He's actually followed in the German press. I was just curious."

"I think he's good-looking, but I was too busy trying not to look incompetent while I was on all fours."

"Wait. You say he appeared ruffled after you said, 'thank you, Kurt?'"

I nod. "Yes, I said thank you. It was difficult, but I think I managed to be sincere. Aren't they polite in Germany?"

"I should have warned you, but this company is a stickler for formality in the workplace. In the Munich office, everyone uses 'Miss,' 'Mrs.' or 'Mr.' to address one another, even the higher-ups. We've had transplants from headquarters. The managers don't even address their secretaries by their first name. That would imply a personal relationship. When they established an office in America, that bit of protocol didn't go well here, so we are an exception. But Kurt is from that culture, so he's probably expecting to be addressed as Mr. Heinrich or Herr Heinrich."

"Jeez, the way he's acting it's more like he is expecting Your High Holiness." Melanie raises an eyebrow. I'm reading slight concern. I redirect the conversation. "I've worked with a lot of hiring managers in the past," I say, attempting to calm her fears, "and most of them were great, but you always have a few problem children. I can do this," I assure her. "I kill them with kindness and dazzle them with results. I usually win them over in the end."

"I know it's crazy, but for the sake of peace, call him Mr. Heinrich, not Herr Heinrich; that could sound condescending since you're not a native speaker. Oh, and pronounce his name with the 'i' long and the last 'h' silent. Like hinrick. It's not the German pronunciation, but that's what he prefers."

I take a sip of my coffee. "Sure, I can do that, Mr. Heinrich it is."

"Look on the bright side: he'll call you Ms. Ivarsson, so you'll still be on equal footing."

I know I look doubtful.

She pushes her untouched coffee to the side and reaches for a folder from her case. "I'm only giving you paper until your computer is ready, then you can pull this information off the SharePoint. I've already given you permission to access this on the server."

"What's this?" taking the paper from her.

"Details about the night crew for the production site. I've already had a call from Matt, asking when you can visit the site. I told him as soon as your computer is ready, which should be today. You have a ten o'clock appointment tomorrow to meet him and tour the production line."

The list of jobs looks pretty standard. If he isn't like Herr Heinrich, I might stand a chance of keeping my job. "Got it, ten, tomorrow. Do you have any advice about Matt?"

Melanie glances around the restaurant, thinking. "He has a charismatic personality," she says, like she is ticking off points on a list. "He's able to get the trust of people quickly. He seems very nice, but he didn't get where he is by not watching the bottom line. As long as you produce, and keep it low-key, you should have no problem with him."

I place the sheet in my folder. "What do you mean by low-key?"

"Around here, we call him Matty Ice, you know, like that quarterback. Do you follow football? I mean European and American. You've got to around here; it will make you seem like one of the boys when Cup finals rolls around and they're all in the lunch room watching a game."

I just look at her, wondering how I got so lucky. I know who Matty Ice is, but she knew him too and now I'll have someone else to talk sports with along the guys around here.

"It's his style of leadership," she continues. "He doesn't like prima donnas or drama. We think it's because of his five-year marriage with that crazed supermodel Jena. She probably burned the drama right out of him. You know she has five memes. Three are from her saying 'please' and rolling her eyes." Melanie demonstrates.

I chuckle. I've seen the memes. Melanie does a scary good imitation of the drama queen of super models. I glance at the paper again. They weren't hiring me to sit on my behind all day. Melanie is closing her briefcase with a snap. "There should be no problem staffing the night crew," I say and smile. < < < < > > > >

About the Author

Pax loves bingeing on fantasy romances, hanging out in her kitchen with friends, and going on road trips when she can get away.

Editing endless business documents for work or ghosting an occasional article was her only writing experience. She made the decision to write fiction about two years ago when she got a wild notion to pen a contemporary romance.

Pax is a California native. She lives and works in Silicon Valley.

Before you go

Thank you for reading *Trinal*. If you enjoyed this book, please leave a review on Amazon, BookBub, and Goodreads.

Stay tuned for other novellas in the **Love at Work** Series
Love Contract
Work Spouse

You might also enjoy:

Sweet and Sultry Series
Someone Like You - Book 1 (Available now on Amazon)
Owe me Something - Book 2

Check the release dates of upcoming books, read excerpts, see author interviews, or join my mailing list to receive my newsletter *Pax World* at paxsinclair.com

Visit me
paxsinclair.com, Goodreads, Amazon Author Central, BookBub
Facebook, Instagram, YouTube

www.ingramcontent.com/pod-product-compliance
Lightning Source LLC
Chambersburg PA
CBHW022040170626
46808CB00003B/1291